"Despite the easy flow of verse, there is a density to this
story with its multiple elements. Lively, moving, and
heartfelt."

Kirkus, starred review

"This novel packs a punch into its shocking and
extremely powerful ending straight from today's
headlines."

Booklist

"This important and recommended contemporary YA
will inspire young people to find their own voices and
take a swing at life. A must-have."

School Library Journal, starred review

swing

Other Novels by Kwame Alexander

Rebound
Solo (with Mary Rand Hess)
Booked
The Crossover
He Said, She Said

swing

New York Times **Bestselling Authors**

kwame alexander

with Mary Rand Hess

BLINK

BLINK

Swing
Copyright © 2018 by KA Productions
Original Art © 2018 by Mary Rand Hess

The art in the book was created using ink and mixed media on paper.

Requests for information should be addressed to:
Blink, 3900 *Sparks Dr. SE, Grand Rapids, Michigan* 49546

Audio ISBN 978-0-310-76192-1

Library of Congress Cataloging-in-Publication Data

Names: Alexander, Kwame, author. | Hess, Mary Rand, author.
Title: Swing / Kwame Alexander with Mary Rand Hess.
Description: Grand Rapids, Michigan : Blink, [2018]. | Summary: "Noah and his best
    friend Walt want to become cool, make the baseball team, and win over Sam,
    the girl Noah has loved for years. When Noah finds old love letters, Walt hatches
    a plan to woo Sam. But as Noah's love life and Walt's baseball career begin, the
    letters alter everything"— Provided by publisher.
Identifiers: LCCN 2018030417 (print) | LCCN 2018038650 (ebook) |
    ISBN 9780310761877 (ebook) | ISBN 9780310761914 (hardback) |
    ISBN 9780310761938 (itpe) | ISBN 9780310761945 (softcover)
Subjects: | CYAC: Novels in verse. | Best friends—Fiction. | Friendship—Fiction. |
    African Americans—Fiction. | Baseball—Fiction. | Letters—Fiction.
Classification: LCC PZ7.5.A44 (ebook) | LCC PZ7.5.A44 Sw 2018 (print) | DDC
    [Fic]—dc23

LC record available at https://lccn.loc.gov/2018030417

Any internet addresses (websites, blogs, etc.) and telephone numbers in this book
are offered as a resource. They are not intended in any way to be or imply an
endorsement by the publisher, nor does the publisher vouch for the content of these
sites and numbers for the life of this book.

This book is a work of fiction. Names, characters, places, and incidents are either
products of the author's imagination or used fictitiously. All characters are fictional,
and any similarity to people living or dead is purely coincidental.

Cover direction: Ron Huizinga
Interior design: Denise Froehlich

Printed in the United States of America

22 23 24 25 / LSC / 10 9 8 7

To the beautiful ones unborn. And
to their forgotten histories.

Prologue

We were halfway through
junior year.
Rounding the bases.
About to score.

Walt was still pretending
like he wasn't weird,
and fronting
cool.

Sam was busy being cool, and *fine*,
while her boyfriend, Cruz,
was busy hitting
home runs
and being president
of the *I'm-so-cool-even-my-temper-is-lukewarm* club.

And I was in the dugout.
Mostly happy
just watching,
trying to get up the nerve
to get in the game.

Things were pretty much normal:
baseball was still king,
but people were also talking about
the American flags
randomly popping up
around town—on car windows at malls,
in graveyards, graffitied
on freeway exit signs.
Everywhere.
Anywhere.

We were best friends
rounding the bases,
about to score.
Everything was copacetic, Walt liked to say.

Until it wasn't.

Part 1:

Cheesecake

Tryouts

We
      go

to
      check

the
      list

and
      for

the
      third

year
      in

a
      row

we
      aren't

on
      it.

I've liked baseball

since I was three,
when Dad handed me
a glove
that swallowed
my arm.
But Walt has loved it.

His trading cards
fill five albums:
Hank Aaron,
Roberto Clemente,
Bryce Harper,
Carlos Correa,
Willie Mays.

He gave away
all his Sammy Sosas.

We've been
to see
the Yankees
at least once
a year.

We love
the hot dogs,
the spin
of a curveball,
the crack
of a well-hit ball.

In our minds
we could hit
anything,
run the bases
like gazelles,
slide into home
safe.

But the truth is
we suck.
Our baseball dream
is a nightmare.
It haunts me.

If only Walt
could catch on
to the signs
the universe
is pitching us,
we could both
move on
from this horror.

Cut

Yo, why are you smiling? This sucks.
Noah, you ever heard of the saying, fourth time's a charm?

It's third time's a charm.
If you'd rather focus on the No, that's on you. I choose Yes.

YES?! What are you even talking about? We didn't make the team. Again. That's a definitive NO if I've ever seen one.
A setback is a setup waiting for a comeback.

Well, you can come back by yourself. I'm done, Walt.
Noah, this is not the time to give up on chasing cool.

I'm not giving up on cool. I'm giving up on baseball. And you should too. We'll find cool another way.
Burger King.

Huh?
Like Burger King, we can have it our way. Don't give up on our dreams.

Your dreams.
I'm not the one who studied up on all the greats in baseball history, and I'm not the one who made his best friend watch the World Series in silence so he could hear the sound of every pitch, hit, and catch. And, I'm not the one who used to want to play catch every day.

Used to.
I'll tell you this, Noah. I WILL make the varsity baseball team senior year. Bet on that. I'll practice harder than before. Work out harder. Get ripped. Give the whole of my heart and soul to the glove and the ball. Become one with the bat. In fact, from now on, Walt's no longer my name. From now on, just call me Swing.

I'm not calling you that.
Well, it's my name. I'm Benny Goodman, yo!

Who's Benny Goodman?
WHO'S BENNY GOODMAN? Are. You. Kidding. Me.

Primer One

Listen to this
clarinet swing,
he says,
playing a song
on his phone.
That's Benny Goodman.
The King of Swing,
the Sultan of Smooth,
the Rambo of Rhythm
and Romance.

Really? Rambo?
Jazz is jungle
and jam, yo!
Plum sweetness
from the first note
to the last,
broken time
put together again.
Benny Goodman is the fixer, dude.

He's sway and swoon,
groove and drive,
melody in your steps,
"Bumble Bee Stomp,"
butter when you talk,
a chance to dance
offbeat,
an in-the-pocket wish
to come true.
Blue wings
that fly you
to the moon
and back.

Oh, well that explains it completely, I say, shaking my head. How'd he die? I ask, knowing he's gonna tell me anyway.

June 13, 1986.
Benny was taking a nap,
snoozing and doozin',
then BAM!
But I guess
if you gotta go,
that's the way
to do it.

I Don't Understand Jazz

While the rest
of the world
listens to trap
and country music,
I'm listening
to Benny Goodman,
and getting accosted
by Walt
and his after-coffee breath.

To me, jazz sounds like
what biting
into a lemon
would taste like
if you could hear it.

I just don't see
the plum sweetness, I guess.

Swing

My best friend
Walt Disney Jones
is obsessed with jazz,
baseball,
dead famous people,
and finding cool,
if it's the last thing
we ever do.

But cool has eluded us
since we met
on the losing-est
third grade baseball team
in the history
of earth.

Cool is Satchel Paige,
the best pitcher
to play the game.
We're just two
juniors in high school
who've struck out
on the field
as much as off.

But Walt's a
self-proclaimed *expert*
on how to
never give up
until you win.

In other words,
he's delusional.
But he is right
about one thing:

Baseball's in my genes, Noah.

His brother, Moses,
is Satchel Paige incarnate,
a baseball phenom
in our town
who got drafted
by the Yankees,
then disappeared into
a sea of camouflage
when he decided instead
to fight
for our country.

But Walt's no Moses,
and neither am I.

Discharged

Mo's coming home from Afghanistan.
YEAH?!

Like this month. MY BIG BRO IS COMING HOME!
WOOHOO!
Perfect timing. Maybe he can teach us how to finally
catch cool. It's exhausting chasing it.

Noah, we're gonna own cool. Like, when people google
cool, a picture of me and you spitting seeds and tobacco
with our hats to the back will pop up.
First of all, I don't chew seeds. And no one chews
tobacco anymore. You gonna eat your fries?

We're destined to make the team next year.
I told you I'm not trying out again. Gimme your fries.

Quit thinking negatively. Don't build more walls to block
what's possible. Crash through, Noah. Crash the heck
through.
Who are you, Oprah now?

It's from a podcast I listen to.
What podcast?

The podcast that is our ticket out of the desert of
callowness. Life is simple, Noah, but you have to use the
miracle power of your mind to tap into the cosmic power
known as The Woohoo Woman.
I have no idea what that means.

It's the secret. If we're gonna learn how women think, we
have to listen to women.

. . . .

23

Truth

Walt knows everything, believes
in the power of anything,

and the stuff he's unsure of,
the stuff he doesn't know, you'd never know,

'cause he's so confident sharing
every idea, tidbit, factoid,

hypothesis, positive mantra
that floats around

in his big ole brain.
I'm not gifted

like him.
Some things, I tell him,

are actually impossible,
like finding

the right words
to tell Sam

she's my archangel,
the one who saves me,

the one who flies
through my mind

night and day.
So, I draw.

Athena Inspires
the Prince

Sing to ... man of twists and t...
driven ... he had plun...
the h...
Ma...
m...
f...

...daug...
...sing for o...oo,

...ll who avoided headlong death
...ome, escaped the wars and waves.

My Secret

In an old
shoebox
under my bed
are drawings
and patchworks
and art pieces
from third grade
'til now.

Baseball bats,
gloves and balls,
starry nights
and moons,
strange dreams,
and hundreds of
hearts sketched
for Sam.

No one knows
about my secret stash.

No one
but my parents
and Walt.

The Dare

The Odyssey, *yo. Really?*
What? It's art.

*Libraries consider defacing a book vandalism and
mutilation. It's a threat to intellectual property. I concur.*
Whatever.

Did you hear anything I said, Michelangelo?
I heard every word you said, Mr. Woohoo Woman!

*It's time for us to know ourselves, conquer our inner cool,
or one day we're gonna end up walking down the street of
possibility, alone, naked, and unhappy.*
Dude, you've lost me. You gonna eat all your fries?

Did you ask her out yet?
Why are you rushing me?

*If 2,539 days is rushing, I'd hate for you to be patient. Yet
do I marvel. Yet do I freakin' marvel!*
She's my best friend. It's delicate. When I'm ready, I'll do it!

FIND a way to tell her, or I'll tell her for you.
No, you won't. YOU ABSOLUTELY WILL NOT TELL
HER!

*Seven years is a long freakin' time not to hook up with your
self-proclaimed soulmate.*
I never said she was my soulmate.

*No, what you said was, and I quote, "Your smile is a joyful
noise that sings to me like a Baptist choir on first Sunday.
So strong, it makes me wanna HOLLA!"*
I said that?

Eighth grade, in Mrs. Allen's class. Killer metaphor, yo!
Oh.

Time to own it, Noah.
Dude, Cruz will kick my—

Assume it won't come to that.
Why?

The day is coming when she'll be available.
Doubtful.

*Yo, have you noticed she's calling you a lot more lately,
wanting to study a lot more lately, generally trying to be
all up in our mix lately? You think that's a coincidence?*
. . . .

*It's not. At worst, she's unhappy. At best, she's unhinged.
Guys like Cruz can throw you off your center. She can do
better than him. It's just a matter of time.*
How do you know all this?

My cousin Floyd.
Your cousin Floyd? What does he know about this?

HE KNOWS EVERYTHING. *He's the one who hipped
me to the podcast.*
Hipped? Who are you, Shaft now?

*Floyd used to date a reality TV star, and he knows a thing
or two about love. Girls are always fighting over him.
I think Steve Harvey was going to do an episode about
him and all his lady friends. He's my romance guru. He
counsels me on my love life.*
What love life?

*The one where I'm going to the prom with the baddest girl
on earth.*
And who is that?

Don't know. Haven't met her yet.
. . . .

Anyway, Floyd is super cool, man.
. . . .

Get in the game, yo!
Yeah, okay.

I think you'll be pleasantly surprised. Let's go see him tomorrow.
Can't tomorrow, I'm helping my mom get ready for her trip.

Then let's go this weekend.
We're going to see my granny.

She lives around the corner from you, yo.
Maybe next week.

You're not getting out of this, Noah. You and me, next week, at Dairy Queen.
Dairy Queen?

That's where he's currently employed.
Wait, he works at Dairy Queen? I thought you said he was cool?

Here, taste this, he says, mixing his bowl of spaghetti with his fries. *You still want a fry?*
. . . .

Next Week

The bell rings.
We all slide out
of our chairs
and rush the doors.

Pretty much everyone else
in my class
casually strolls
to their car,
or a friend's car,
to drive home, or to a job,
or to get some eats, while
lucky me
still gets to mad dash it
to the bus.

Except for today.
Walt's been harassing me
for a week to meet
his cousin.
So, today, I'm going to Dairy Queen.
Today, I'm getting schooled
on romance
by a romance guru
who works
at Dairy Queen.
Today, we're supposedly
coming up with a plan—at Dairy Queen—to
finally
tell my best friend
of seven years
that I think
I love her.

While I'm waiting

for Walt
by the flagpole,
baking beneath sun
hot as the equator,
someone walks up
behind me,
covers my eyes,
and whispers
in a voice
smooth as silk:

Guess who?

Surprise

Sam, Walt, and I
used to hang
every day
after school.
Skipping rocks.
Walks to the lake.
Video games.
Homework.
Just kicking it.
Granted, that was
middle school,
but still, we had fun.
Together.

Ever since
we got to high school,
she's all new—classes
and friends.
I mean, we still hang,
but it's always
on her terms,
mostly baseball games
to see Cruz play,
and sometimes
we study together.
Well, she studies.
I listen to music
and crack jokes
with Walt,
and pretend
my heart isn't beating
like hip-hop,
and my stomach

isn't all jumbled
like heavy metal.

Like it is
right now, right
now it is like
jumbled metal, right now
a heavy pain
jumbled
into metal, heavy
in my soul like metal
waiting to be
unjumbled. Right now.

My Funny Valentine

You know what today is, Noah?
Wednesday.

You're hopelessly unromantic.
. . . .

It's Valentine's Day.
Oh. Why aren't you with Cruz?

I'd rather be with my bestie, she says, grabbing my hand,
not knowing her teasing is torture.
. . . .

Hey! What are you doing?
Waiting for Walt.

I just saw him in the gym.
Really? We're supposed to be meeting.

*I guess he's trying to get fit. You know, you could buff up a
little too, Noah. I mean, if you want to impress the ladies.*
I'm not interested in impressing girls who just want guys
with muscles.

*Spoken like a guy with no muscles. Come on, my car's this
way. We're going shopping.*
Shopping?

Emergency. I need you.
Okay, but I gotta wait for Walt—we got plans.

*Walt can wait. Plus, you guys are spending too much time
together, and I'm a little jealous.*
You're the one who's always busy, Sam.

Just text him. We can hook up with him later. C'mon, let's ride.

What are we shopping for?

For correct grammar.

Whatever.

Dresses. We're shopping for dresses.

. . . .

Unforgettable

Cruz may get
to be her boyfriend
every day,
but today,
right now,
I get to see her
glide out of
the dressing room
in every color
prom dress imaginable.

I get to see her
stun.
I get to see her
spin
like a whirling dervish.

I get to see her
look crazy beautiful
in every single one
of the fifty-some dresses
she tries on.

I get to see her strut out
in the red one
with the strap
off the shoulder,
the one
that makes my heart
freefall,
like an eagle diving
off a canyon.

The one that makes me realize
that I am way out
of my league,
and no amount of baseball
or Dairy Queen
will ever get me
in this game.

You okay, Noah?

Insults

You like it?
Yeah, it's okay, I guess, I lie.

Sucknerd.
Toadlip.

Horsehead.
Big butt.

Big butt? That's all you got? You lose.
Seriously, the dress is tight as your cornrows.

Awww, that's beautiful, Noah. Nothing like a new dress and a best friend to get rid of the blues.
What's going on?

Cruz is kinda putting pressure on me.
Pressure? What do you mean?

What do you think I mean? Did you know female dragonflies fake their own deaths to get out of relationships with male dragonflies?
You're scaring me.

How do I tell him to slow down?
Just tell him no.

I'm scared he might break up with me.
Then it wasn't meant to be. Choose the YES that's best for you.

Huh?
Never mind. So, you're wearing this dress to the prom?

Maybe. You think Cruz'll like it?
I guess.

Are you going?
I don't know.

You didn't ask anyone yet? NOAH!
I'm weighing my options.

Michelle said she thinks you're kinda cute.
I don't need you to be my matchmaker, Sam.

Testy, testy! I'm just trying to help.
Plus, it's my mom's birthday, so I'm saving my cash for
a nice gift. Next year I'll get the limo, the tux, do the
whole thing.

Hard to argue with a guy who thinks about his mom.
You're a good guy, Noah. Too good.
What does that mean, too good?

Just means some girl is gonna be lucky to get you.
. . . .

Let's keep looking.
I thought you chose the red one. Haven't we seen enough
dresses?

Just a few more. Then we can go to the game.
The game?

Cruz has a scrimmage today.
Yay!

We sit

in the top row
of the bleachers
like we own the field,
drinking Fanta,
eating hot dogs
and salted pretzels
before the game
starts.

The players
on both teams
cross their arms
over their hearts
for the anthem,
in unity.
I get up
to do the same,
but she pulls me
back down.

What are you doing?
We're taking a stand, Noah.

Actually, we're sitting, I say.
Exactly.

Why?
If you don't stand for something, you'll fall for everything.

Everything's not political.
*Actually, everything is. You either uphold the status quo,
or you see what's wrong and try to change it.*

. . . .

Hey, look over there. Isn't that ironic? she says, pointing
at the two police officers

removing
the cluster
of flags
lined up
like tombstones
along the outfield fence.

Stars and Stripes

Like people
in uniform,
flags salute
everywhere
you look.

They wave,
reminding you
this is America.

They're the biggest news
to hit our town
in years,
subject of news broadcasts,
letters to the editors,
Sunday sermons,
and daily gossip.

Is it something suspicious
or patriotic?
Littering or
liberty?

*It could be a terrorist or extremist group distracting us,
mocking us before an attack*, one of my classmates said
last week.
Who cares, another one offered.

I say nothing.
Are they really hurting anyone?
I mean, it's the flag.

To me, it's all just
kinda insane,
because no one can agree
on why the flags are here,

who's planting them,
and whether or not
we should be
happy or offended
that they're growing
like dandelions.

Batter Up

After an inning
of near-perfect pitches,

Cruz struts
up to bat.

Sam wiggles
in her seat,

bending forward
with a burst of pride.

He hunches
his upper back,

shimmies
his front leg,

ready for a hit
that'll send the scouts

chasing his tail.
I hate that his swing

is so slick,
catlike.

Smooth like velvet
then lightning fast.

But he misses.
YES! I scream to myself.

Sam hides
her face

in my shirt
then peeks.

He misses again.
C'mon, babe, she whispers. *He must be off tonight.*

It happens, I say, with
a little burst

of my own pride,
and hope

that he strikes out.
But he doesn't.

He SLAMS one
to Jupiter

and everyone starts
jumping and shouting,

and the face
that was in my shirt

seconds ago
is now

in the air
screaming, *GO, CRUZ, GO!!!*

He slides into third base.
At least it wasn't

a home run, I think,
faking a smile.

A Lonesome Ride

After the game,
Sam and Cruz
take off
like lovers
eloping.

I hop
on a bus
by myself,
single
and discouraged.

On the way home,
I sit
in the last row, stare
out the window,
imagining
the static stares,
the glares
from people
wanting to know
why I haven't
told her
how I feel.

Did the old guy
sporting the applejack hat
and bushy mustache
just look up
from his newspaper
and shake his head
in disgust
at me?

The sign above
my seat
reads *In Emergency Break Glass.*

This is an emergency.
I feel broken.

Why haven't I told her? WHY HAVEN'T I TOLD HER?!
Why haven't you told her? the old man asks, in my head.
*And don't even think about breaking that window. It's
illegal. A federal offense.*

So is loving someone
for this long
and not doing something
about it.

Phenomenal

Samantha "Sam" Worthington
is a dancing, swaying, prowling contradiction.
She is tough and kind.
Confident and uncertain.
Grounded, but if she had sparrow's wings
she'd soar off and probably never return.
She does whatever she wants.
To borrow a line from a book we read last year,
She's a woman, a phenomenally phenomenal woman.
She sparkles.
And I've been seeing stars
ever since third grade
when Zach Labrowski—the bus patrol, the dictator
of the big yellow kingdom on wheels—
told me to get out of his seat and I wouldn't.
So he punched me.
I was the new kid who didn't know The Rules.
Out of nowhere came Sam.
She pushed Zach Labrowski
out of the seat, then
squeezed in next to me
and offered a tissue
'cause apparently there was a tear.
Or maybe a couple.
Her eyes were like two fiery sunsets,
full of warmth and concern,
and I kinda knew right then I would love her
for the rest of my life.

Phone Conversation

Yo, what happened to you?
My bad, Walt. I kinda got sidetracked.

Who's Walt?
Huh?

The name's Swing, remember?
Oh yeah, well, I'm sorry, Swing. I got caught up in
something else.

*Successful people jump at opportunity and take
advantage of it.*
Stop with the podcast stuff. It's stupid.

Actually, that was Sir Mix-a-Lot. I saw him on Ellen.
. . . .

So, why'd you bail on me?
Sam and I went to the mall.

*WOOHOO! Are you serious? Why didn't you lead with
that?*
It was nothing. We just talked, and I helped her pick out
some dresses for prom.

*Wait, you helped your soulmate pick out dresses to wear to
prom with her boyfriend? On Valentine's Day, no less?*
. . . .

*Are you even aware of how ridiculously muddled that
decision was?*
Look, it all happened so fast.

*You're fastly becoming her forever friend, and once that
happens, there's no upgrade available.*
Upgrade?

Friendship is like the Great Wall of China, dude. Once it goes up, you're never getting to the other side.
. . . .

We really need to go see Floyd. It's getting crucial.
Tomorrow.

Tonight.
Seriously, I just got home, and I haven't eaten yet.
And, Ms. Miller gave me until midnight to turn my paper in.

Trivial details. We will eat at Dairy Queen. Ms. Miller extends extensions all the time. Just tell her you've been stressed 'cause your parents are going to Barcelona and you'll be alone.
I guess.

Spain

Each year,
the International Hotel Association
holds their week-long conference
where hotel managers
talk about hotels
from sunup
to sundown,
then get drunk
and post videos
of horrible, late-night
karaoke sessions.

This year,
it's in Barcelona.
My parents
were chosen
to represent
the local chain
of hotels
they manage,
and they're staying
an extra three weeks
to celebrate Mom's birthday
on a twenty-one-day European cruise
they asked me to join them on,
and which I politely declined
for obvious reasons.

La Quinta

*Yo, let's get a luxury suite at La Quinta and have a
party. Throw the biggest jam of the year.*
How about there are no luxury suites at La Quinta.

*Doesn't matter. We can do a poolside party. I'll DJ,
try to get my Aunt Barbara to make mini-quiches and
wiener rolls.*
How about NO.

*What's the point of having hotel moguls as parents if
you can't floss?*
They manage three hotels—they're not moguls. Plus,
nobody's ever flossed at La Quinta.

*C'mon, Noah, they're gone for, like, a month. In the
history of child-rearing, nobody's parents have ever left
for a month. This is a historic moment. The universe is
saying yes to us. We must represent for all kids, or this
may never happen again. Ever.*
. . . .

*We must fast track cool. We must throw the dopest party
imaginable.*
Not happening.

Your loss.
I can accept that.

I'm on my way. Be ready.
Fine.

Tattoo

Walt is sloth slow
when it comes to
going somewhere,
primarily because
of his hang-ups,
or superstitions;
like he can't walk
up or down
the same side of the street
on the same day,
or in and out
of the same door
when he's coming
or going somewhere.

Today is no different.
I sit and wait, until
my gangly best friend
walks up in a muscle shirt
with no muscles,
wearing
throwback headphones—playing
jazz, no doubt—
and something
dark and blue
affixed
to the skin
on his left shoulder.

Inked

WHAT. IS. THAT?
I got a tattoo.

When?
When you bailed on me earlier, he says, peeling away
the wrap to reveal . . . WHAT THE?!

Dude, if you were going for the Tupac look, you
missed terribly. They left off the *T,* and you need
them to fix it ASAP before you get roasted over an
open pit of hell at school come tomorrow.
*Nah, bro. It's not a mistake. I didn't want THUG Life.
I wanted—*

HUG Life? Have you lost your mind?
*I haven't. I am more enriched today than yesterday.
Woohoo Woman has taught me more than I ever
dreamed I could know about life and—*

Did your mom see it?
*Not yet, but my new soon-to-be, almost stepfather did.
He took me to get it. We're bonding. Hug Life. Get it?*

You've gone overboard.
*You must embrace life with a metaphorical hug, and
sometimes a literal hug, to really squeeze the life juice,
the goodness, out of living.*

I'm done.
*No, we're just beginning. Dairy Queen, here we come!
Wanna hug?*

Dairy Queen

Walt struts in
like this whole thing—
our whole life—
is a movie.
And he's the lead.

He orders
a garden salad,
chili cheese fries,
plus a Cappuccino MooLatté
like he's ordering
vodka on the rocks.

Please, don't mix all three.
Please, don't, I say to him.

His cousin Floyd swaggers
in from the back
with a smile
bigger than Orion,
locks that nearly drag
the floor, and
two huge front teeth
as white as the shake
freezing my brain.

He takes a few orders,
makes a few cones,
then sits down
across from us
and starts nodding
like he's the principal
and we just
got sent
to the office.

Walt begins to talk,
but Floyd shushes him,
waves his finger,
closes his eyes,
and starts tying his hair
into a bun.

Apparently, weird runs
in this family.

Conversation

Floyd's got dates tonight, so let's giddyup. What's up,
little cousin?
Everything's copacetic, Walt says.

I see you're still wearing those pop bottle glasses. Didn't I
tell you, the ladies only dig them if they're fresh?
I'm working on it, Floyd. I'm saving my paper for some
nice frames the chicks will love.

Hold on there, partner. Floyd cannot school you on your
feminine consciousness if you're using that language.
Ladies, women, yeah, but never, EVER chicks. That's
sexist. Tell 'em, kid, he says, looking at me with one eye
open.
Yeah, I guess, I say.

My bad, Floyd.
You still listening to the podcast, right?

Indeed.
Good, 'cause that's the textbook to a richer life for ya.
Those sisters are preaching the gospel! The heart of a
woman beats like a raindrop on a crag. You understand,
right? he says, looking at both of us with his eyes wide
open now. I nod my head, pretending like I do.

I heard there's a wedding. Floyd didn't get an invite, but
Floyd may crash it. You pumped, little cousin?
Her guy wants me to be his best man.

Well?
It's peculiar at best. At worst, creepy.

Do you like him?
I don't dislike him.

You talk to Uncle Albert?
I haven't talked to my dad in months. He's got a girlfriend in Texas.

Giddyup, then.
. . . .

Your future stepdad is a lucky man. Aunt Reina was always fine as full-bodied wine.
. . . .

. . . .
. . . .

What? It's not like Floyd's trying to Oedipus your mom . . . Anyway, what's up with you guys?
I keep telling my best bro, Noah here, that he needs to hear from you how to talk to a chi—woman. From a real-world romance guru. He's got the love for her, but he can't tell her. The words get in his way.

Dig it. Just call Floyd Casanova.
June 4, 1798. Died in a library. Was reading a book, then BAM!

Huh?
He knows how famous people died, I say.

Real talk, cousin?
It's a gift.

Like anybody?
Anybody famous, infamous, or noteworthy.

How about Bob Marley?
He was playing soccer, and he injured his toe.

He died from a toe injury? C'mon, really?
No, but they found a cancerous growth on the same toe, and then it spread to his brain and lungs, and then BAM!

That's so random, but intriguing. Marilyn Mon—
Uh, I gotta get home soon, I say.

Right. Sorry, Noah, my dude. You've come to the right
place. So, tell Floyd about this young lady.
What do you want to know?

How does she wear her hair, what kind of music does she
listen to, any piercings, name of her perfume, last book she
read, vanilla or chocolate, how she makes you feel—you
know, the crucial happenings in her day-to-day world?

This Is What I Know about Sam

She laughs, I smile
from ear to ear.
She smells so good,
I can taste it.
She cries and I want to make everything better.
She raises an eyebrow and I quiver.
She loves mint chocolate chip 'cause she's sweet.
She wears her hair like a queen.
She walks—

STOP! CUT! C'MON, SON, he screams, with a frown
and a smile at the same time, turning customers' heads
toward us. *Cliché, Cliché, Cli-freakin-ché! Okay, look, this
is how you need to see her. Like she's a living, breathing,
walking manifestation of art. Pay attention to Floyd . . .*

This Is What Floyd Knows about Sam

She laughs like a whip-poor-will sings.
She smells like honeysuckle in summer.
She cries like a soft and delicate rain.
She raises one eyebrow like a rainbow perched on heaven.
She loves mint chocolate chip because it's got that kick.
She wears her hair like freedom and it captivates you.
She walks like a wave, assured and ready to carry your
heart in hers.

Yeah, I say. That's what I meant.

The Secret Formula

He closes his eyes again,
looks like he's back to meditating,
then mumbles something
incomprehensible about
training wheels
and grabs my hands
like we're both in prayer.

Okay, this is what Floyd thinks you ought to do . . .

Unlock your heart

Take this key, he says, squeezing my hand
so hard my knuckles crack.
Open the door to your destiny,
crash through it.
Enter the house.
Own it.
Own the farm
and the ranch, cowboy.
Saddle up.

Huh? I say to myself, wondering what the heck he's
talking about.

This is your movie, Noah.
Write a new scene
in her life.

Paint her a new world.
A strong one, that holds
her hands,
brings the light,
makes the darkness cease,
and captures delight.

Do not let your lips become bricks,
your fingers an anchor,
your heart a desert.
Shout it from sea to sea.
She is a wave,
large and looming,
but Floyd will not let you drown.

Paddle for the wave.
Catch it.

Ride it.
Ride it as long as you can.
Right into daybreak.
Unpack your cool,
take the training wheels off,
ride with her love.

Cruise like fire in her sky.
You got that? he asks, opening his eyes, finally.

Yeah, I lie. 'Cause I don't. Got that.

At all.

Guru Confusion

That was some mind-blowing counseling, was it not?
If by mind-blowing you mean absurd and perplexing,
then it sure was. And why was he speaking in third
person? That was weird.

He's eccentric.
He's confusing. I have a headache from all the
metaphors. And, what's up with the training wheel
stuff?

It's the podcast. He's the producer of it.
He produces the Woohoo Woman thing you've been
talking about?

I told you he's a guru.
This just got weirder.

You just gotta listen to it, and you'll COME ALIVE.
I'll send you the link later tonight. WOOHOO, he
hollers, as we cross
the street
to avoid
being on the wrong side—the block
he can't walk on.

We turn down
a winding road
that makes the walk home
extra, extra long.

Yeah, thanks for your help, I say.
You're very welcome.

I was being sarcastic, Walt.
So was I.

A Sign

Spray-painted
on a stop sign
near his house
is a red-white-and-blue
lone star
with one word
underneath it.

America?

The Meaning

Why the question mark, though?
*Has America lived up to its ideals? There's a debt to be
paid and it's time to cash the check. Let America be
America. For all. What's in your wallet, Noah?*

You got all that from a question mark?
I'm just saying, the flags are a sign.

Of what?
Of things falling apart.

Your brain is like a mashup of everything you've ever read
or seen or heard.
Hey, I'm just being real.

Somebody posted they saw someone in a white sheet
putting the flags up.
What, like the Klan?

Nah, like a ghost literally disappearing into the darkness.
*My soon-to-be stepfather thinks Amazon's behind it. Some
kind of big advertising thing they're doing.*

To sell flags?
Maybe they're making a play for the US Army?

That's ridiculous.
*Why? I mean, they own everything. The end of the world as
we know it, and it starts with Whole Foods and drones.*

Real profound, Walt.
*Just real, my man. You want profound, listen to the podcast
tonight. Mind-blowing stuff, Noah. Mind-blowing.*

I don't know if I'll have time with homework, shower,
and my stomach is cramping up from the milkshake—
Noah, love does not wait.

Come to think of it, why are you so obsessed with my love life?
Or lack thereof.

Whatever.
Ubuntu.

Huh?
The philosophy of Ubuntu is, I am because we are. I help my brother, I'm a better person. Simple as that.

You really think Amazon is the apocalypse?
Nah, my soon-to-be stepfather's an idiot.

Family Meeting

When I get home,
I find Mom and Dad
sitting quietly
on the living room sofa,
eyes frozen
on me,
like they're about to drop
some seriously bad news.

I'm not sure
if someone's lost a job,
if someone has died,
or if they're pissed
because I came in late
on a school night, or forgot
to do something I was
supposed to do.

All I know is
when there's a family meeting,
it's usually something grim,
and it begins with . . .

Sit Down, Noah

Is everything okay?
Did you forget something? my dad asks.

I put the recycling out.
Yep.

I should have told you all I was going to be out late
tonight. I'm sorry.
It's just the considerate thing to do, Noah, my mom adds.

Today was an important day too, Mom says, while Dad
winks at me like a madman, and I wonder, did I forget
something significant?
*Still is important, honey. Still is. Noah, don't you have
something to say to your mother?*

Happy Valentine's Day, Mom, I say, and kiss her on the
cheek.
And? Dad says to me.

Uh, annddd—
Happy Birthday, Mom, Mom says, shaking her head and
laughing.

Oh yeah. I remembered, then totally forgot. I'm sorry,
Mom. Happy Birthday, I say, walking over to her,
ashamed.
Thank you, honey!

I feel like a real butthole.
You should, Dad says, as Mom slaps him on the leg.

Noah, she says, *we're leaving for Barcelona in a few days.*
Yeah, I know.

And there are some house rules you'll need to adhere to.
I think I'm clear on all the rules, you guys. No parties on

weekdays, no more than nineteen people in the house at a time, and no beer on an empty stomach, right?

. . . .

Look, guys, I'm good. I'll check in with Granny every day. Meals are labeled in the freezer. I'll mow the lawn on Saturday. No one is allowed in the house, and so forth and so on.

Now that we've gotten that straight, Dad says, *let's talk about the dent in my car.*
What dent?

Follow us, my dad says, leading me to the garage.
Oh dang.

The Walk of Death

Mom, Dad, and I walk
to the garage
like we're heading
to a funeral.

Mine.

Dad loves his
Volvo.
He's had it
since I was in
middle school, and
takes pride
in the fact
that it has never
had a scratch,
is always polished,
and that it sparkles brighter
than a lake
in summer.

We're real quiet
walking to the garage.
My mind is racing
through the one time
last month
he let me drive it
to school.

Did I dent it
getting gas, or
did a rogue shopping cart
hit it
at the mall?

Go ahead, open the garage door, Dad says, shooting me a stern look and giving me a little shove.

I'm screwed.

Twins

There's a TV preacher
who lives
in our city
named Pastor Mike,
whose kids go
to my school.

Every now and then,
we see him cruising
around town,
always with his wife, Becky,
holding their two bassett hounds,
William and Faulkner,
who hang out the passenger window
of his shiny, candy-apple red
Ford 250 pickup truck
with 35-inch-tall tires
and a license plate
that reads
ROM 12 9.

My granddad had
the same truck—same
color, only older,
dirtier, and smaller,
with 16-inch baby tires—that
has been sitting
in the driveway
of my granny's house.

Until today.

Two-of-a-Kind

What's this?
It's yours, Noah, Mom says. *Don't you love it? Granny
doesn't drive it, so she gave it to you. We fixed it up, put
some new tires on it, and voilà, you have your own car to
drive around. It's kind of sporty, like you.*

I stand back,
catch my breath.
First of all,
it's not sporty,
and if this jalopy
is the truck
that is supposed to look like
my kind of car,
I'm in trouble
with life.

Yeah. It's cool. Really, really cool, I say, wishing my
acting skills were better.
How is it that it's my birthday, and you're getting the gift?
Mom says, kissing me on the cheek.

I have something for you too, Mom, I promise. I just
need to pick it up.
Yeah, right, Dad says, jangling the keys, then tossing
them to me. *Let's take it for a spin, give it some get up
and go.*

The Jalopy

We *spin*
and sputter
around
our neighborhood streets.

There is no get up.
Or go.

I want to be grateful.
I want to be thankful.
But I'm embarrassed.
I hope no one drives past us
and waves.

What are you going to name it? Dad asks. *Sam?*
I laugh and say, Maybe, just to be agreeable.

But I would never
name it Sam.
It's not hot
and it absolutely
has no style.

At least Pastor Mike has rims
and booming speakers
that blast
his sermons.

The upholstery
above my head
is torn and tattered.
And, beneath my feet,
the bottom might literally fall out
at any second.

I think I'll name it Granny, I say.

Good plan. Make sure you call her tonight and thank her,
Dad says,
picking up
the sun visor
on the passenger side,
which he doesn't think
I saw fall
into his lap.

Three-way Conversation

Guys, I got a ride.
WHOA! A NEW CAR, BRO?
A truck. New to me.

That's awesome, Noah.
Thanks, Sam.
YO, CAN I GET A RIDE TO THE MALL?!

Walt, how about we let him enjoy the moment first.
WHO'S WALT?
What are you talking about, Walt?

TELL HER, NOAH, Walt hollers.
And, why are you screaming? Pipe down, fella.
He doesn't go by Walt anymore.

Oh, really, Sam says, rolling her eyes through the phone.
The name's Swing.
Swing? How'd you come up with that?

Tell her, Noah, he says again.
Nah, you tell her, Swing.
'Cause I'm hitting it out of the park next year. That's why.
Baseball, girls, cool.

Good luck with that, uh, Swing, Sam says.
So, guys, I do need to get my mom a birthday gift. So
maybe the mall—
OKAY, I'M ON MY WAY OVER!

Nah, man, tomorrow. We just got back from Dairy
Queen. I can't go back out tonight.
*Wait, y'all went to DQ without me? You know how much I
love a dipped cone.*
You don't really hang with us like that anymore, Walt says
to her, nonchalantly.

Seriously, guys.
AM I LYING?
· · · ·

We had a meeting, Sam, I say, trying to make things a little less awkward, even though Walt's right.
A meeting? About what?
· · · ·

Helloooo! What kind of meeting?
JUST A MEETING, SAM. MEN TALK!
You're an idiot, Walt.

Uh, guys, I gotta run, I say. My dad's calling me.
YEAH, I GOTTA GO TOO! I SENT THE PODCAST, NOAH.
What podcast?

· · · ·

You guys are acting real strange. This isn't finished, jokers.
LATERS, SAM.

Text me later, Noah.
Uh, okay, Sam. Walt, after Sluggerville, let's hit the mall tomorrow.
Don't leave me out. I'm going too.

You sure Cruz won't mind?
He's my boyfriend, not my boss, Walt. Geesh, guys, why are y'all trippin' all of a sudden?
· · · ·

WE JUST WANT BETTER FOR YOU, SAM.
Boy, bye!

First Attempt

I'm gonna do it.
I'm gonna sit down
and write her a new world,
maybe a love song
or a sonnet.

I'm gonna write it
like a boss
like I'm Bru*Noah* Mars.
Tell her exactly
how I feel,
channel the love wizard, Floyd,
and make her swoon.

I scratch the pen
against the paper,
but nothing
appears on the page,
just spirals and spirals
of spinning anxiety.

My mind's a blank
block of cement
and my palms
a sweaty swamp
of nerves.

In desperation,
I turn to
a couple
of women.

WOOHOO WOMAN Podcast #1: Who's at the Controls?

Do you want better? Better friends? Better jobs? Better kids? Better Love? Better you? Better YES? And less NO in your life? Then you've tuned in to the right place. I'm Jackie, and I'm Marj, and this is The Woohoo Woman Podcast.

JACKIE: *WOOHOOO!*

MARJ: *We're back for the last half hour of* Woohoo Woman, *hopefully with a little less profanity in this segment.*

JACKIE: *Forgive me, listeners, I get a little excited when it comes to saying yes to life. Let's be honest, being a Woohoo Woman in today's world takes nerve. Sometimes it takes brashness. It always takes bravery and the managing of careers, dreams, ambitions, family, romance. IT'S REAL OUT HERE IN THESE DAYU— In these streets.*

MARJ: *Breathe in and breathe out, girlfriend.*

JACKIE: *Okay, let's get back on topic. What were we talking about, Marj?*

MARJ: *A man is a woman's partner, but not her necessity. It is a choice. The Woohoo Woman needs a man to understand that the way to a woman's heart is by listening, and . . .*

JACKIE: *And by admitting that we can be brilliant and beautiful, independent and hot, at the same time. And if one more man whistles at me when I'm walking to my car, I'm gonna go all Wonder Woman on his as—*

MARJ: *Assuming that men are listening to us right now, I'd like to offer this to our brothers . . .*

JACKIE: *We want our men to love us for our dreams and choices. We want them to hear us. We are much more than legs and lips. The Woohoo Woman is much, much more.*

MARJ: *We are explorers of life. A world within a complex* *world. Our controls aren't just on and off. They're more like a keypad to a space shuttle on its way to another galaxy.*

JACKIE: *We are the friggin' space shuttle, Marj. We control the controls.*

MARJ: *Woohoo!*

JACKIE: WOOHOO!

MARJ: *That's our time for today, sisters and brothers. Time to wake up and find your Woohoo! Check us out at WoohooWoman.com for more podcasts, and to read our manifesto on what we stand for. Any last words, Jackie?*

JACKIE: *Do the friggin' work, women. Holla!*

MARJ: *Next week we're playing an oldie but goodie.*

JACKIE: *One of our producer, Floyd's, favorites. We're taking the training wheels off and poppin' wheelies! So tune in to* The Woohoo Woman Podcast.

For Your Safety—Please Read All Warning and Operating Signs Before Batting

We're here
under the big lights again
with the smell of sweat, old shoes,
sugary bubblegum,
and gasoline-scented breeze.

Children run around
everywhere, and though the sign says,
No Pets Allowed,
dogs bark,
scavenge for food
off the ground.

I could be sitting
in the designated "dugout"
where parents
and tired friends go
to chill
on benches and eat snacks
when they're bored,
but instead, I stand
behind the chain-link fence
doodling
on a vintage baseball ad
I found
in a magazine
on the ground,
while watching Walt
miss
and miss
and miss some more.

He sways back and forth
on the artificial turf
with a sparkle of hope
in his eyes.

Today is the day magic happens, he says, readying
himself. *It's Swing Time!*

The sound of ball
hitting aluminum
in every lane
but his.
The protective screens
shaking
with the vibration
of each hit,
or in Walt's case,
each miss.

*Mo once told me in a baseball swing, you gotta use a toe
tap or leg kick to gather momentum.*
Yeah, I've seen that. Why don't you try it! I say, feigning
encouragement.

Swing repositions
his pose,
and I'm not sure he knows
what twists where,
or how to kick
while simultaneously hitting
the ball.

He has plans
for a line drive,
to crush it,
slash it,
slay it.

But in truth,
if this were a game of ducking,
he'd win.

He is getting a little better,
hitting at a slightly higher percentage,
though it would take
a mathematician
or his patient best friend
to notice, because
he has been so bad
for so, so long.

When his bat
finally meets ball,
it scatters off far right,
hits the barrier.
Walt spins around
in celebration,
grins like a crescent moon.

I'm in it to win it, Noah. Barry Baby Bonds in the house!

And though I'm slightly tired
of watching, I shout,
Keep your eyes on the ball, Swing. You got this!

Because part of me hopes
he does.

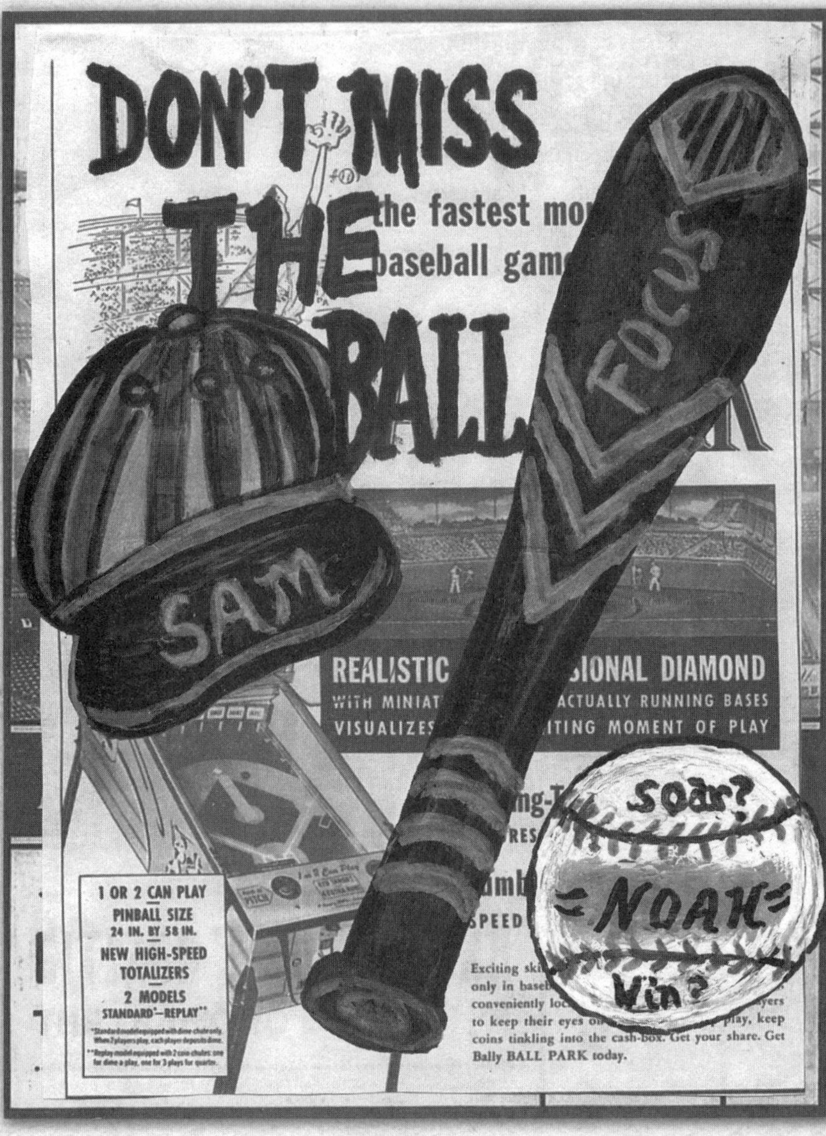
DON'T MISS THE BALL
the fastest mo
baseball gam
FOCUS
SAM
REALISTIC
SIONAL DIAMOND
WITH MINIAT
ACTUALLY RUNNING BASES
VISUALIZES
ITING MOMENT OF PLAY
Soar?
NOAH
Win?
1 OR 2 CAN PLAY
PINBALL SIZE
24 IN. BY 58 IN.
NEW HIGH-SPEED
TOTALIZERS
2 MODELS
STANDARD*—REPLAY**
SPEED
Exciting ski
only in baseb
conveniently loc
yers
to keep their eyes o
play, keep
coins tinkling into the cash-box. Get your share. Get
Bally BALL PARK today.

Conversation on the Way to the Mall

You text Sam?
I guess there's no USB in here.

Dude, did you let her know to meet us?
Chill, bro, she's coming. We need to pimp this ride.

. . . .

I guess we'll just listen on my phone.

I already listened to the podcast. Don't really get that
Woohoo stuff.
It was kind of layered, Noah.

So, you didn't understand it either.
I did. They were talking about listening, and Wonder
Woman.

And don't forget space shuttles. That's a lot of metaphors.
You need to listen as much as possible. You'll catch on. I've
been tuning in for months, and look at me.

I'm looking and I'm not impressed.
We need to think like them so we can understand them.

So, we need to listen?
Basically.

The mall

is overrated,
plus, I don't have
enough money
for a mall gift,
so we head
to a thrift shop
Walt knows about.

In my vintage ride,
we listen to more Woohoo
to get me pumped up
to finally tell Sam
how bold
and brave
and beautiful she is.

So, you're gonna finally do it? he asks.
Probably, I say, not convincing him. Or me.

Cruel Comparison

We pull up
bursting with
Woohoo warrior spirit,
but there she is,
standing outside
HIS car,
holding on
to HIS arm.

We walk toward them.
I look down
at my own arms
and then over at Walt's.
It's like we're competing
for the skinniest hanging noodles.

I rise up
high as I can
in my high-tops,
cross my arms
and push out my biceps
with my knuckles.
Anything not to feel so
small.

Cruz

has a full beard
that would make
hipsters jealous
and guns the size of
a wrestler's.

He drives fast,
pitches fast,
and has baseball scouts trying
to keep up
like lost puppies.

Freshman year,
he tormented us,
called us ladies,
but last year
when he and Sam started dating,
he stopped.

Now, he calls us *Hey you*.
It's like all the good in him
just rushed to the front
of the line,
and he got all new.
Sam has a way
of doing that—bringing out the better
in you.

Out With the Old

is the name
of the thrift store,
which smells
like perfume
and mothballs.

If you added onions,
it'd be like lit class
with Ms. Miller,
who smells
like all three
when she leans in
with hot breath
and recites
Shakespeare.

To be or not to be: that is the onion, Walt likes to say.

I laugh,
thinking about Ms. Miller
among the dizzying
racks and racks
of used clothes,
old books and records,
handmade jewelry,
weird pottery duck mugs,
frog ashtrays,
and other decades-old knickknacks.

Hey you, what's funny? Cruz asks,
popping up
from behind a rack
of old, wooly coats
with Sam's arms
enveloping him.

Conversation

Nothing, really. Good game yesterday.
That's how I roll, he says, not looking at me.

*HEY, NOAH, WHAT ABOUT THIS FOR YOUR
MOM?* Walt screams, wearing a big ole purple church
hat. I ignore him as he holds up several more.

Look what Cruz is gonna buy me, Sam says, holding up a
shiny heart bracelet. So cliché.
Babe, you're my heart, he says, and they kiss like nobody
and everybody's watching. So cliché.

*Stop, babe, we gotta help Noah find a birthday gift for his
mom.*
YEAH, WHY DON'T Y'ALL GET A ROOM, Walt yells
out, from over by the one-dollar used books.

I gotta go, babe, Cruz, says, kissing her again. I try not
to pay attention to how long it lasts—eleven seconds—or
how his hands move up and down her back (slowly), or
how her eyes are closed and his are looking at—
Hey you, stop staring at my girl's haunches.

Haunches? Really, Cruz, Sam says.
What? I know how you don't like when I say—

Boy, bye. Have a great practice.
I'll see you tonight, babe, he says, knocking over a stand
of knickknacks, not picking them up before walking out
the door.

There's literally nothing and everything here. Let's just
go back to the mall.
Do you have an idea of what she'd like? Sam asks.

Something my mom could take on her trip would be
cool, I say, helping pick up the mess Cruz left behind.

What about the hats and bonnets that Swing was holding up?

Kinda corny and ancient.
VINTAGE IS THE NEW BLACK, NOAH, Walt hollers.

I can't see her wearing those hats, I say.
What about, like, a purse or a scarf?

She doesn't wear scarves.
So, a purse it is.

Yeah, I guess that could work.

I follow Sam over
to the register
where the jewelry is,
and point to a bag
that matches
some of her luggage.

Nice taste, Noah. Look at you, she says.
What?

EXPENSIVE TASTE TOO, Walt yells. *If it's in a display
case, it's gonna be pricey, yo.* He walks over to eye it.
*Oh, I know all about these. Fancy people carry them to
show other, less-fancy people that they're rich . . . LIKE
REALLY RICH.* He leans down to peer into the case.
How much does it say it is? Sam asks.

*IT'S ONLY TWO HUNDRED NINETY-FIVE
DOLLARS*, Walt says, stressing the ONLY part and
laughing.
How much was that purple hat again?

Gift Giving 101

Sam tries to explain to me
that you can tell a lot
about a man
by how he treats
his mother
and that I should consider
buying the bag,
because when it comes
to my mother,
money shouldn't be an object,
and if the gift will make her happy,
I should get it.

*You mean like the bracelet Cruz is buying you—will that
make you happy?* Walt asks, sarcastically.
And that's when
she realizes
he left
without buying it.

YOU GOT PLAYED, SISTER, Walt says, laughing from
over by the bookshelf. *When a guy shows you who he is,
believe him,* he adds, shaking his head, and looking at
me.

Sam immediately calls Cruz,
and all we hear
is her fussing
as she storms
out of the store.

The Keepall

As I stand there
eyeing the purse,
wishing I wasn't broke,
a girl
with retro frames
and long, braided black hair
with matching nail polish
walks over,
takes it out the case,
and sets it on the counter.

It's Louis Vuitton, she says. *It's called a Keepall bag. At two hundred and ninety-five dollars, it's a steal.*
Striking. Exquisite, Walt says, looking not at the bag, but at her.

In the 1850s, Louis Vuitton was the packer for the empress of France. That's how he got his start. Packing the suitcases for Napoleon Bonaparte's wife.
May 5, 1821. Napoleon died from stomach cancer caused by ulcers, Walt interjects. *Got way too stressed out from being a traitor and whatnot, and BAM!*

Random, right? He knows how people died, I say to the girl, because I know she thinks we're crazy.
It's a gift, Walt says.

Impressive. But it wasn't that Napoleon. It was the nephew, Napoleon—
Napoleon the third, that's right, I knew that, Walt interrupts again, looking a little embarrassed. *Kidney disease, bladder stones, chronic bladder and prostate infections, arthritis, and obesity, then BAM. Died on January 9, 1873, which is coincidentally the birth date of*

the Jewish poet Hayyim Nahman Bialik, who died from prostate cancer. Bladders are no joke.

Impressive, the girl says to Walt again. *As for the bag, it's a beauty. Vintage and classy,* she adds.
Like you, Walt says, walking over. *I'm Swing.*

Divya. I'm sure we can work out a deal. You shopping for someone special?
Yeah. My mom, I say.

Sweet.
His name is Noah, Walt chimes in, throwing a pea-green, itchy-looking scarf around his neck. *Divya's a charming name, ambrosial even. What does it mean?*

Divinely brilliant.
Your eyes are brilliant, a divine mix of swirls and color. Like there are two worlds spinning behind your glasses. Wait, did I just say that out loud?

You did. And thank you.

He grabs her hand
with a confidence
I've never seen
in mixed company
and kisses it.

He. Actually. Kisses. Her. Hand.
And it's so corny
it's actually cool.

She smiles.

So, do you want the bag?
He can't afford it, Walt says.

I can speak for myself, dude. Uh, I can't afford it.
I can offer a fifty percent discount.

He still can't afford it. But if you got dishes, he can do your dishes, or he can dust, Walt says, laughing.
Hey, can't you loan me the money? I whisper to Walt.

Yeah, Mr. Swing, why don't you loan your buddy the money to buy a gift for his mom? It's the righteous thing to do, Divya says, looking him straight in the eye and not blinking once.
I don't make loans, Divya. Especially to friends. Remember, Noah?

C'mon, man, I'll pay you back.
How? With what? You don't have a job.

My parents are leaving me with some loot before their trip.
Hmmm. Let me think for a minute. He starts handling the shirts and old hats and gloves like a miser. *Maybe I'll loan you the money.*

That would be so cool. That would be the coolest thing you've ever done for me. Like, seriously, the coolest.
Shall I wrap it up, then? Divya says.

Not just yet; there's stipulations. You got a piece of paper I can borrow? He'll need to sign something.

. . . .

The Loan

Payment is due
the first Friday of every month.

Car rides
whenever I desire.

Missed payments
mean a penalty fee

of five dollars.
And there's interest:

twenty-five cents
on the dollar.

Sign
Here.

I walk outside

the thrift store
with the Keepall
in hand, wondering
if I've signed a deal
with the devil's
accountant,
when I see Sam
put away her phone,
and wipe away
her tears.

Everything okay?
*Yeah, he just told me the reason he didn't get the bracelet is
because he wanted to surprise me.*

And you believed him? Walt asks.
*He's gonna come back and get it for me. He really is
thoughtful, guys.*

Yeah, and forgetful, Walt says, shaking his head.
*You got the bag?! Nice! Smart move, Noah. Y'all want ice
cream?* she says, yawning.

Somebody needs a nap, Walt says.
I'm good. Let's hit DQ?

NO, we both say, immediately.
I'm kinda in the mood for frozen yogurt today, I add.

By the way, Sam says to Walt, *the tattoo is dope, but I
think they left a letter off.*

After dessert

I drop Walt off
and take Sam
home.

My hands grip the wheel
like I'm barreling
through a storm.

She leans her head
on my shoulder,
her face against

my body,
giving me
chills

and a warmth that
snakes around
in my stomach.

She makes me
want to
tell her

how good
it feels to . . .
how much

I really want to
let her know
I love

the way she
has me coiled,
completely

tongue-tied,
all the way down
to the gas pedal.

Conversation with Walt

I didn't sleep at all last night.
Why?

I couldn't stop thinking about her.
Who?

Divya.
Who is that?

Seriously, yo. Divya from the thrift shop.
Oh.

I'm captivated. She was quite pleasant.
Apparently ambrosial too. Whatever that means.

I think she's into me.
I didn't get that at all.

I need to come up with a plan.
. . . .

And you do too. You gotta step up your game.
I will.

*Noah, the universe is conspiring to give you everything,
but you gotta do your part. This isn't a game of Yankees
versus Orioles. This is a game of love and war.*
I will.

*You said that today, yesterday. And the day before that.
And last week. And last summer, and the summer before
that. And the five summers before that. When you two
went to the same Jesus camp . . . and when she saved your
butt in third grade.*
I SAID I WILL!

Just write her, like Floyd said, if you're too afraid to tell her to her face. Pour out your heart completely so she has no choice but to fill it.

Well, I did kinda write her something last night, after I got home.

Share

Okay, but don't laugh.
No judgments here.

It's a song or something. It's called *A Song for Sam.*
Bwahahaha . . .

Nah, never mind.
*Sorry, man. I'm sorry. I'm not laughing AT you, I'm
laughing WITH you.*

I'm not laughing.
*Oh, right, well, my bad. It's just you can probably come
up with a more original title. Okay, I'm listening, I'm
listening.*

First Draft

I want you
to be
my symphony.
My own
private symphony.

Your moist lips
the oboe
my tender mouth
sings through.

Your legs
two piccolo trumpets
blazing through
the air.

Your hips—

Whoa, WHOA, BOY! Noah, maybe we should go see
Floyd again. You can't send her THAT.
Why, what's wrong with it?

For starters, it's mildly stalkerish, and you use the word
moist. For seconds, it's just vulgar. C'mon, yo, turn off the
Showtime and HBO. Don't go all Netflix on me. PBS with
a splash of Lifetime, maybe. Women are much more than
legs and lips. You really need to listen to more Woohoo
Woman.
Maybe I'll work on it.

Maybe, uh, start over.
Yeah.

But first, let's hit the library.
Why?

There's gotta be a book that can help you with this.
What kind of book?

Writing for Dummies.

Woohoo Woman Podcast #3: Training Wheels

Do you want better? Better friends? Better jobs? Better kids? Better Love? Better you? Better YES? And less NO in your life? Then you've tuned in to the right place. I'm Jackie, and I'm Marj, and this is The Woohoo Woman Podcast.

JACKIE: *Welcome, welcome, loyal Woohoo listeners. Today, we are talking about taking those training wheels off and popping wheelies. What do you say, Marj?*

MARJ: *So, I'm trying to get my son to pop off those training wheels, but he's a little afraid. I keep telling him he's ready. He just needs a little faith. Easy for Mama to say, right?*

JACKIE: *It's a highway out there, and no one's breaking for ya. You must be ready to put your foot to the metal . . . give it a little gas and GO!*

MARJ: *Leave it to Jackie to mix the metaphors in a jiffy. From bicycles to Corvettes.*

JACKIE: *Either way, we're spinning. Going round and round, trying to get from can't to can, from no to yes. And sometimes we can wait too long, and our "training wheels," as it were, become a crutch. Know what I'm saying? "Life is a highway . . ."*

MARJ: *WOOHOO!*

JACKIE: *I was a little off-key.*

MARJ: *Maybe a little. But I love that song. Hey, Floyd, crank up Rascal Flatts for us.*

JACKIE: *When do we know we're ready to take that chance in life and go for what we want?*

MARJ: *New career. Follow those dreams we've been hiding in our hearts for years. New man. New move. A trip around the world. We must take risks to gain, and we must* *have faith that, even if we have to slam on the brakes, we'll get back on the road and drive.*

JACKIE: *That's the problem for me. Knowing when to brake and when to accelerate.*

MARJ: *And sometimes I wonder if I pass on those anxieties to my son.*

JACKIE: *No time like the present to give it your all, Marj, and show your little man that you're his hero. You are a wondrous woman. A Woohoo Woman full of potential.*

MARJ: *Thanks, Jackie. And that's why we're friends. You are full of metaphors and encouragement. I feel like now's a good time to tell you something.*

JACKIE: *What?!*

MARJ: *I've been dreaming of becoming a . . .*

Next time on The Woohoo Woman Podcast, *find out what Marj has been dreaming of "becoming," and then we'll be interviewing love expert from Cupid's Corner, Amy J, who has advice on how to find and keep lasting love in a world that feels like* Where's Waldo.

What Matters

As soon as I drop Walt off
at Sluggerville,
I turn off the dreadful podcast
and focus my attention
on the only Woohoo Woman
who matters right now: my mom.

Inspection

Except for a
a tear
and spots
of blue ink
on the bottom,
her gift
is in good condition.

It smells
like must
and nostalgia,
so I dust it out,
clean it gently
with a damp rag.

I feel something
at the bottom,
lumpy, thick,
beneath
a tear
in the fabric.

So I lift it,
and discover
postcard-sized,
fading envelopes
scattered
underneath,
faintly addressed
to someone
named Annemarie
in Pennsylvania.

I count
five envelopes.

Lucky Day?

I've heard stories
of people
finding big bucks
in books
and trunks,
between sofa cushions,
behind paintings,
inside old purses.

Maybe today is my lucky day.

I carefully open
the first envelope,
and shake it.

Nothing comes out
but dust.

And a letter.

dear love,

five minutes after we met, my smile exploded. when i told you i
wanted to paint u from floor to ceiling, a masterpiece, u laughed
like a river. or volcano. and then u walked away with ur friends
& my whole life stopped.

i couldn't breathe, until u turned around, came back over & gave
me the note.

i remember the way ur auburn hair fell down ur back, i
remember ur laugh dancin up my spine, i remember it all, even
fats waller playing on the record player when you walked in.
i've got a feeling i'm falling, an ocean floor, a buried treasure. i
want to discover you again!

remember me to harlem,

corinthian c. Jones.

p.s. annemarie, excuse my misspellings & the failures of my
new typewriter. i am still learning to type & it seems that only
"J" will capitalize.

dear love,

thank u for coming to see me once again. it means everything. i have known
u for mere months, but it feels like u have been a part of me since creation.
when u were here last, u were sweeter than the wine we drank, more lovelier
than the trumpets blazing through sugr hill. it has felt like more than two
thousand seasons since we laughed up in our magical place.

i have busied myself with ur portrait, which i hope to finish by summer, as i
have finagled my way into a summer teaching gig at lincoln. yet, i'll be 30 miles
from where my heart resides, where each and every breath is always with
u. the bad is that i'll have less time to ponder, less time to paint at will &
whimsy. but regardless of what i'm doing, or where i stand, i see you—
everywhere. it's love that fills my eyes. u are my first thought at first sight.

there is a Jazz showcase coming up in a month's time. will u come? u can
bring your friends again, if it is easier. if we are to keep up appearances.
i Just need to carry you in my arms like a wave carries ships to faraway
lands. i Just need to kiss u inside the daze of my dreams, inside the blue
Jazz. i Just need u and your loyalty, ur truth, and your abundance
of light. i am not picky how we manage. ur pure essence may be both
blessing and curse, but how do i not love wholly & solely when the mere
parting of ur lips swallows me whole. takes all

that is in the chambers of my heart, and soul, captures my breath? i beg
you . . .

come, swim with me in this deep blue unknown.

corinthian.

Text to Walt

8:52 pm
I just called you.
You still at batting cages?
Hit me back when you finish.
My world just got ROCKED.

Tonight, after reading the love letters

I decide I'm ready
to come alive,
to write love
on the page
like it's a new language.

Tonight, I'm ready
to tear courage
out of the book of dares
and make it mine.

Tonight, I'm ready
to draw her lines,
tempt her to walk across
the Grand Canyon
of my love
and not look down
in fear.

Tonight, I'm ready
to capture her heart
like a monarch,
set her free
to come back to me.

Tonight, I'm ready
to build a fortress
of promises
that can be ours,
our castle of dreams.

After reading
the love letters
from Corinthian
to Annemarie,

I think
I'm ready
to take the chance
and go for what
I want.

I think.

Bon Voyage

My parents' flight
leaves at 11:00 pm,
so the official birthday party
with French vanilla ice cream
and Oreo cheesecake,
Mom's faves,
is quick and
sweet.

Dad gives her
another elephant—this
one from South Africa—to add
to her prized collection
of elephant statues
from around the world
that have overtaken
our whole freakin' house.

She smiles
when I give her
the bag,
devoid of dust
and letters,
and filled
with all kinds of
travel accessories:
sleep goggles,
romance novels,
and a penciled mélange
of self-portrait styles
so I can carry you near my heart, she says, crying like
I imagine
all moms do.

I kiss her goodbye,
Dad kisses me,
then she grabs me
like she's never
going to see me
again.

Noah, be good. Be careful. Use good judgment, and . . .
Mom, you act like you're flying to Pluto. It's just Spain.
Try to have fun and not worry.

It's just that we've never left you for this long.
I left you. Fourth grade. Wizards and Warriors Camp.

But, it wasn't a month.
Felt like it.

He'll be fine, honey, Dad says. *My mother will be here
with him for a few weeks.*
Guys, I'm a grown man now. I'll be fine. Now, go.

And with that,
I shove them
out the door
to their taxi,
so I can get back
to the old letters,
to my new life.

Text from Walt

7:30 am
I'm intrigued. Fill
me in Monday, yo.
Mom's freaking out
over the wedding. Got
me on lockdown
all weekend: cake tastings,
invitations. I'm planning
my escape, though . . .

Star Spangled

On Monday,
school explodes
when the admin finds
a ginormous flag
wrapped around
the big tree
out front,
and a dozen smaller ones
graffitied
on the sidewalk.

People mull around,
not sure
if they should be scared,
or proud.

The school is locked down.
Nobody in
or out,
so we sit
in the car
and wait.
And wait.

And I show Walt
two letters.

He reads

them, and
I swear
I see a tear
sneaking from
his right eye.

Then, a smile.

*These letters are stirring. Genuine heart-melting stuff. You
found these in the bag?*
Yep, there were five of them.

Why you holding out on me?
They're at home.

I think this is a sign, yo.
For what?

For you to paint her from floor to ceiling.
. . . .

It's time, he says, *for you
to take
the training wheels off.
Time to take your feet
off the brakes
and put the pedal
to the metal.
You gotta paint
your masterpiece, Noah.
You gotta ride
into daybreak.
You gotta tell Sam.
Today.*

I know, I say, and for once, I actually believe myself.

120

Part 2

I Guess I'll Hang My Tears Out To Dry

Too Good to Be True

After almost a week
of solitude,
a week of revving up
the grit
and guts
to tell Sam
the deal
but wimping out,
guess who shows up
at my front door
with a Star Wars sleeping bag,
a bat,
and a suitcase
filled with
eccentric fixations
he says bring him luck—action figures,
black soap,
vitamins,
and essential oils
for my well-being.

IT'S TIME TO SWING, NOAH!

What are you doing here?

The weight should be on the balls of your feet and your knees should be slightly bent.
Huh?

In order to have a balanced swing, you gots to have a balanced stance. I've been working on my stance. The weight should be on your back leg. If your feet are too close together, you'll have a difficult time keeping your head level.
It's pretty obvious you're not level-headed.

Baby Bonds in the house! My swing's gonna be lethal, Noah.
Again, what are you doing here?

Still drama at my house. My future, soon-to-be fake dad is back in town for the week, and he's staying with us. Not a good look.
You don't like him at all, huh?

I don't dislike him. But I need to keep him on edge. Make sure he knows I'm just not gonna let him act any old way. He's gotta earn my compliance. And this right here is a start, he says, dropping what looks like a gift card down on the table in our foyer.
What's that?

The price for my love.
A gift card?

A two-hundred-and-fifty-dollar gift card. All-you-can-drink coffee. WOOHOO!
First a tattoo, now this.

You gotta pay to play, yo!
Cool, but, what does this have to do with you being here?

124

A bunch of aunts are at the house helping my mom
plan the wedding. It's gonna be in our backyard. A lot of
familial shenanigans I want no parts of.
Is your brother home?

Not yet. Like next week, he'll be here.
That's so cool. I wonder what he's like now.

He's got a beard. He sent pics. But he's still the same. Can
I bring him to the party?
What party?

I have plans for us, and they are going to enlighten you,
my man.
I'm not interested. And, you really can't stay here.

If your grandma shows up, I'll hide in the pantry, or the
closet, or the bathroom until she leaves.
I need my privacy.

Hey, remember those letters you showed me? I need more.
I'm galvanized.
Are you even listening?

First we celebrate, then we read the letters.
Celebrate?

We're celebrating your enstoolment.
That sounds disgusting.

The Master and the Pupil

You're the king of the castle now. Can't you feel the tinge of freedom in the air?
No, I cannot.

We've just been given the keys to a museum that houses the rarest Egyptian artifacts.
Huh?

Responsibility, Authority, Freedom of mind and body. Yo, LET'S DO THIS!
You just left Starbucks, didn't you?

Yep.
You told your mom you're crashing here?

Of course. I told her you need help watching the house. You good with it, just for a few days, while we plan?
Plan what?

The first thing necessary in teaching is a master—the second is a pupil capable of carrying on the tradition.
Let me guess, you're the master?

It's time to let love rule.
And how do we do that, master?

Today, Swing teaches the King how to throw the dopest party imaginable.
That's not going to happen.

It's already happening, he says, laughing this sinister laugh, then dropping his belongings down and walking into the kitchen.
I can't throw a party.

Well, I already texted Sam, and she's already spreading the word, so do you wanna rethink that?
. . . .

126

Hey, let's get to those love letters. I can't get them out of my head.

Walt, turn around and go back home.

It's time, Noah. IT. IS. TIME.

It is not time.

We kick off

our bachelor life
eating leftovers,
listening to a podcast
called *Straight, No Chaser,*
and watching
the police chief
on the news
promise
to investigate—
and possibly prosecute—
the flag litterer,
who, in addition
to defacing public property,
is now suspected
of breaking
and entering
a Walgreens.

I thought they were open twenty-four hours, Walt says.

Then, I let him
read
the rest of
Corinthian's ancient
love letters.

6 november 1966

dear love,

yr father is not going to keep us apart. i miss u. a fish in water.
a soul stranded. in the big sea. the world is changing and i know
it will take years of undoing the white robes and old ways, but
my love is stronger. let us not dwell on what's not, rather on
what is. me. you. us. together. one day.

forever,

corinthian c. Jones.

12 november 1966

dear love,

i painted u again. then i went to church with nothing but a penny
for an offering. inside i prayed a thousand prayers sacredly
and secretly holding the memory of yr hand in mine. yr voice
echoed in the old organ that played our song . . . because all the
mysterious and magnificent things that make music will be
ours under notes of heaven above and earth below. our
love provides god's angels with trumpet and song. does it
matter that the world wants to keep us apart? when i think
of harlem, i think of u. when i walk to the street corner to buy
apples, i walk with u. when i dance, i dance only with u. when
i prime a canvas, it is always u taking shape. i look for your
luminosity in the colors. u are the purples, yellows, and reds.
every shadow is u sweeping the room, sweeping the streets.
when i dive into dreams, there's u. everywhere is u. then us.

even though i've lived here many years prior to us,
remembering those days seems pointless up until u entered
my life, gave me everything, like the goddess of muses. heaven
may be a place where artists go when they die, eternally
playing songs, painting scenes, writing plays, or else napping,
but i regret to inform the big man that i'm not leaving for
eternity until u and i can be seen as an "us" on this same
earth.

yours,

corinthian c. Jones.

17 november 1966

dear love,

they could not keep harriet tubman from freeing my people.
they could not keep reverend king from that bridge in selma.
and not one or ten or one hundred shotguns will keep me from
harrisburg. from seeing you. we will figure out a solution. all
the answers are in love. thank you for Jumping into my loving
arms at the train station. but it was not smart to hold my hand
on your front stoop. i know you are strong and unafraid. it is
what chains me to you, but as my grandma liked ta say, a blind
mule ain't afraid of darkness. whoa annemarie. we will have our
chance to sway and sing and kiss and dance. we will gallop with
the butterflies and honey bees, you swinging in and out of my
arms on the breeze. our samba will be rhythmic and alluring
and deep.

for now, i love staying up all night and finding orion and
pretending our love exists in zion. these are the only things that
matter. copper sun and alabaster moon. they each need each
other. we need each other. each day without u is as blue as the
sky. let us not be apart too much longer. until that time, like the
song says, i guess i will hang my tears out to dry.

remember me to love,

corinthian c. Jones.

p.s. my great-grandmother was cherokee, which means i've got
an eighth of indian. that part of me will always protest this
holiday, but i wish you a plump turkey and holiday greetings.

Ebony and Ivory

Where's the rest?
That's it.

What?! You can't leave me like that.
I didn't leave you like anything.

You sure there's no more letters? You checked the bag?
Thoroughly?
That was it, Walt.

Well dang, yo.
I know. I wondered what happened to them too. I even
googled him.

Anything?
Only that some dude named Corinthian Jones, who
was *born* in 1966, was about to "turn up and sip a little
drink." According to Twitter.

These letters are slightly mysterious. It's like a TV show on
paper, and we're binge watching.
It's kinda wack, though, to be eavesdropping on their
love. Maybe this isn't cool.

What's not cool is her pops pulling a shotgun out and
trying to keep them apart.
True, but why?

Seriously, Noah.
What? The dad could be keeping them apart for any
reason.

He was from Harlem in 1966. And she was in Harrisburg,
PA, which is not exactly Harlem. Paul McCartney and
Stevie Wonder, yo.
Huh?

Ebony and Ivory. There were those who didn't want black people dating white people back in the day.
I thought Corinthian was Cherokee.

And this is why you keep getting Cs and low scores on your PSATs. You need to read. Really read the letter and think about the time period and the context and the meaning.
You're doing the most. Now you sound like Ms. Miller, and that's just not cool. I did notice Corinthian had some good lines though.

Goddess of muses.
That's the one! That's exactly how I feel about Sam.

Then use these letters as inspiration. Be like Corinthian and go for what you want, no matter the cost.
. . . .

Or do nothing, I really don't care. I'm hungry. What're you cooking for dinner?
I'm not cooking for you.

Let's get pizza and beer.
We don't drink beer.

Then just order pizza. I gotta go work on my stance.

Texts with Granny

9:43 pm
Hey, Granny.
Just checking in.

9:49 pm
Granny, it's Noah.
Things are good over here.
You okay?

9:49 pm
YOU DON'T NEED TO
CHECK IN SO MUCH.

9:49 pm
Huh?

9:52 pm
ARE YOU OKAY? IS THE
HOUSE OKAY? YOU
HAVE ENOUGH FOOD?

9:52 pm
Yes, Granny, but why
are you screaming?
Turn your caps off.

9:54 pm
I DON'T KNOW HOW
TO Do oh wait did that
work noah????????????

9:54 pm
Yes.

9:57 pm
noah, i don't want to

134

stay over there
any more than you
want me to stay

9:58 pm
over there, so how's
about you don't
burn down the house,
you don't have any

9:59 pm
wild parties, and
you come see me
weekly to check in
'cause i'm a little

10:00 pm
busy with senior dance
and book club
and netflix.
have you seen

10:01 pm
luke cage? too violent
for me, but the crown
is omg. also,
me and the girls

10:02 pm
are going to the casino
for the weekend.
if you won't tell,
i won't tell. DEAL?

10:02 pm
So you mean . . .

10:04 pm
I WAS DRIVING
A SCHOOL BUS
AT YOUR AGE.
YOU'RE OLD ENOUGH
TO START TAKING CARE
OF YOURSELF.

10:05 pm
Okay. Well, I'll call
you every day to
check in.

10:07 pm
NOT NECESSARY. I'M
IN AND OUT
THESE DAYS, NOAH,
WITH MEETINGS

10:09 pm
AND DANCE, YOU SEE?
JUST CALL ME
if you get thrown in jail.

10:09 pm
Okay. Well, I love you.

10:12 pm
Granny?

10:12 pm
Janice Wallace has left the conversation.

Inspiration

In the still of the night
I take one of
Corinthian's letters,
retype
his story
of love
as if it's my own.

I begin
with his words,
trace a heart,
make them mine,
borrow
his love story,
wonder if it
can repeat itself,
wonder if Sam
can love me
like Annemarie
loved him.

Friday Morning

Howdy, sunshine.
How's the stance?

*Didn't work on it as much as I should have. Got distracted
with some very important research.*
What class?

Divya 101.
Seriously?

*Those letters, yo. They got all up in my feelings. The
unrequited love. The romance. I think I'm in love.*
With the letters?

*Keep up, Noah. With Divya. I want to know everything
about her.*
What'd you find out?

She's an older woman.
How old is she?

Nineteen, according to my research.
I think you're out of your league.

Yo, why does the kitchen smell like Sharpie? he says,
pouring chocolate milk into a bowl of cereal and
blueberries. *And what's with the mess in here? It looks like
Times Square on New Year's Eve. How long you been up?*
Not long. Rereading the letters, drawing a little, trying to
get inspired to take the training wheels off.

Well, good for you, he says, slurping his concoction next
to me at the counter. *Let me see.*
It's just scribbles and stuff.

Let me see.
Nah. Don't want to share.

Don't want to share. What? Is it another sappy, crappy
love song?
Nope.

Then hand it over, he says, grabbing one of the pages I've
been working on for hours, before I can pick them all up
off the counter. *Let's see what we have here.*

Practicing

YOU DREW THIS FOR SAM?
No, not *for* her.

You know what I mean, dude. WOW! This is not just drawing. This is game-changing, paradigm-shifting-ish stuff, Noah!
Floyd said paint her a world, or something like that.

Dang, you did the thing. What is this, some kind of postmodern, collage mashup love letter?
You're crazy, bro!

I'm serious. I don't know what you call it, but it's dope.
It's mixed media.

I mean, I knew you could draw, but this is next level. Who's your influence?
Who's my influence?

Yeah, every great artist has another artist who inspires them.
Picasso, I guess. Lately, I been looking at a lot of art by Romare Bearden.

You know he played baseball.
He's an artist.

Yeah, but before he was an artist . . . I think this is the universe calling us, Noah.
Huh?

In his previous life, he was an amazing pitcher in the Negro Leagues. He played for the Tigers and got recruited by the Philadelphia Athletics, but he didn't accept their offer.
Why?

They wanted him to pass as a white player.
Why?

*'Cause America is crazy like that sometimes, especially like
fifty years ago. He never played professional ball again.
Instead—*
He became one of the most talented collage artists of all
time. That's pretty cool, Walt.

You ever been to any exhibits of his work?
A bunch. Online.

Not online, like in person?
We don't have any museums around here.

There's a bunch of museums.
Like two hours away.

*Ever heard of a bus or a train? Or your new truck? C'mon,
Noah.*
I can see all the Picasso and Bearden I want thanks to
Google.

Not the same as an exhibit.
I saw some art in person, when I was little. I think I went
to a children's museum. I remember they had a lot of
naked animal sculptures.

Wait, aren't all animals naked?
My point is, I've been to a few museums. But Google is
my friend.

*Dude, you think Miles Davis just listened to recorded
music? No, he snuck into jazz clubs when he was fifteen.
He listened to jazz live. LIVE!*
. . . .

You think Picasso googled for inspiration?
I doubt he had WIFI.

*You get my point. If you want to be an artist, you need to
see art. Up close and personal. Originals. Hold it in your*

third eye. Smell it.
Smell it, huh?

I've been to opening day of the Yankees every year for the past twelve years. You know why?
'Cause your uncle got you tickets?

You're exhausting. Your proclivity for not hugging life is just exhausting.
So, like you were saying, you think this piece of art is dope? I ask, holding up my masterpiece.

Very. You gonna show it to her?
NOPE! One step at a time. I was just messing around.

I thought you were gonna tell her today.
Maybe tomorrow.

Saddle up, Noah, it's time to go surfing.
I'm guessing that is another metaphor, because we live a hundred miles from any body of water.

The wave's a-calling, my dude.
Yeah, well, so is school. We're outta here in fifteen minutes. Be ready.

A Clue?

As we pull up
to Starbucks,
Walt sees
this old musician
trumpeting a song,
and collecting money
in an old instrument case
that has an American flag
affixed to it.

Maybe he's our flag guy?
I've seen him before.

Really? Where?
*Kinda looks like Dizzy Gillespie. I saw him once outside
the thrift store, then I saw him near the batting cages.*

Who, Dizzy?
No, *him*, he says, nodding toward the homeless guy with
the big cheeks blowing the horn.

Hey, Youngbloods, the man says, *y'all want a song?*
You know any Dizzy Gillespie? Walts asks.

*Youngblood, that's like asking Nelson Mandela if he knows
freedom.*
*December 5, 2013, anti-Apartheid icon, freedom fighter,
human rights activist, father of modern South Africa.
After twenty-seven years of wrongful imprisonment, after
walking out of prison a free man to thunderous applause,
after becoming president of South Africa, he succumbed to
tuberculosis, respiratory infection, and old age. And, BAM!*

Amen, says the trumpet player, who then starts playing a
tune, a tribute.

Patriot

That's Hugh Masekela, Walt says. *"Grazing in the Grass."*
That's the one, the old man says.

The name's Swing. Nice to meet you.
Robert, says the man.

You from around here? I ask.
I'm from everywhere. I like to say my home is vast and includes eight continents.

. . . .

The eighth one being the largest and the hardest to get to. I sleep where my feet land.

Wait, didn't I see you by the thrift store a month or so ago?
Ahhh, the thrift store. I found these new-old shades to keep the sun out of my eyes, he says, lifting the frames so we can see his big, bug eyes.

You get the flag there too? Walt asks, thinking he's being clever.
I collect a lot of stuff out here on the road. Somebody gave it to me.

I'm just asking 'cause we've had some drama.
Oh yes, I heard. Flags stirring up a heap of something in the people. Like I say, when you get lost, let the music find you. A little bit of jazz might save this place.

I couldn't agree more, Walt says, smiling and nodding in agreement.
You get on stage, you gotta have respect for all the musicians around you—sax, drums, keys, bass—even if you don't like 'em. You like their sound. What they bring. So, you learn to work together. This world is big enough for us all to play in one great orchestra.

144

That's deep.
That's Wynton Marsalis, Youngblood.

. . . .

I'm Noah, I say, to fill the awkward silence.

Do you know who gave you the flag? Walt asks. *Did you*
see the person?
I have seen someone. But I can't say who. Could be you.
Could be me. Could be anybody.

Could be Herbie Hancock, Walt says, with a smirk.
What you think you know about Herbie Hancock? he says,
laughing big and wide, his gapped white teeth front and
center.

He's in my top five, for sure.
You got Herbie on keyboard?

I got Oscar on keyboards. Miles on trumpet—
Bird on saxophone. Ella singin'—

And Herbie as bandleader.
Youngblood, you alright with me. As for the flags, I can't
help you. Could be you. Could be me. Could be anyone.

What does that mean, "could be anyone"? I say.
Look, Youngblood, the flag means a lot of different things
to a lot of different folks. But the one thing it should mean
for everyone is freedom. Mind, body, and soul. Red, white,
and blue. America the beautiful. The greatest love story
yet to be. Remember this, love gotta always win, gotta be
sincere. Hate that which is evil, and hold fast to everything
that is good and righteous, ya hear me?

I hear you on that, Swing says, looking at me.

I stand there,
caught up in

145

his words,
wanting to say something,
but not knowing
what.

He clears his throat.
His eyes sparkle,
but his forehead crinkles
with a seriousness
that speaks volumes
all on its own.

He puts his lips
to trumpet,
puffs out
his cheeks,
and all the
patriotic notes come
spilling forth.

America the Beautiful!

The line

is too long
at Starbucks,
so Swing skips
his coffee.

In class, he wears
his old headphones
made sometime
in the 1900s.
Wears them proudly
like they're the latest
Beats or Bose.

He's napping
during study hall
with the volume
way too high.

Primer Two

Can't skip my latte, Noah. Deadens my woohoo.
You're awake?

Just resting my eyes.
Um-hum.

Listen to this, he says, putting the headphones on me.
What am I listening to?

Tell me what you hear.
Jazz music, I guess.

Listen to it. Really listen to it, Noah. Let it envelop you.
Seep into you. Then, tell me what you feel, my dude.

. . . .

Park of Love

I don't know, I guess
I feel like I'm at a park,
running from slide to slide,
climbing ladders,
hanging upside down,
swinging on the big swings,
eating ice cream,
ending the day with a mad kiss
under the jungle gym.
That's kind of how the song
makes me feel.
This is a song
about living it up
with your crush.

Right?

WRONG!

Walt says, laughing out loud.
Honest guess, though.
It's a tune called
"Your Feet's Too Big."
It's literally about
someone's feet being too big.
Fats Waller made it famous.
Died of pneumonia December 15, 1943
going cross-country
on a Super Chief train.
VROOOOM, *then* BAM!

After the Lecture on Jazz

I see Cruz
and Sam
in the hallway,
entwined
in love.

She kisses him
loudly and
my eyes sting
with the noise of it.

I try to slide by
unnoticed.
But I can feel her
catching up
to me.

Noah, stop! she calls out. *I need to talk with you. It's
important.*
I turn around. You okay?

I don't know.
Did something happen?

Meet me for lunch.
In the cafeteria?

No.
Where?

Meet me at your car. We're eating out.
But I brought my lunch.

Bring it with you then.
Where?

Pizza Inn.
Okay.

A Big Hiccup

We sit
across from each other
drinking
flat sodas,
eating
cheap buffet pizza
so dry,
it gives us both
hiccups.

I stare at her,
wonder
if she knows,
if Walt told her,
if she sees
into my sappy soul
and realizes I'm
a silly, lovelorn
sap.

She reaches
into her purse
and hands me
a manila envelope
like it's top secret.

Why are you acting all *Mission: Impossible*, Sam?
Look at this, Noah. OMG, look at this, she whispers as I
open it.

Written at the top
in block letters
is:
To: Sam
From: X.

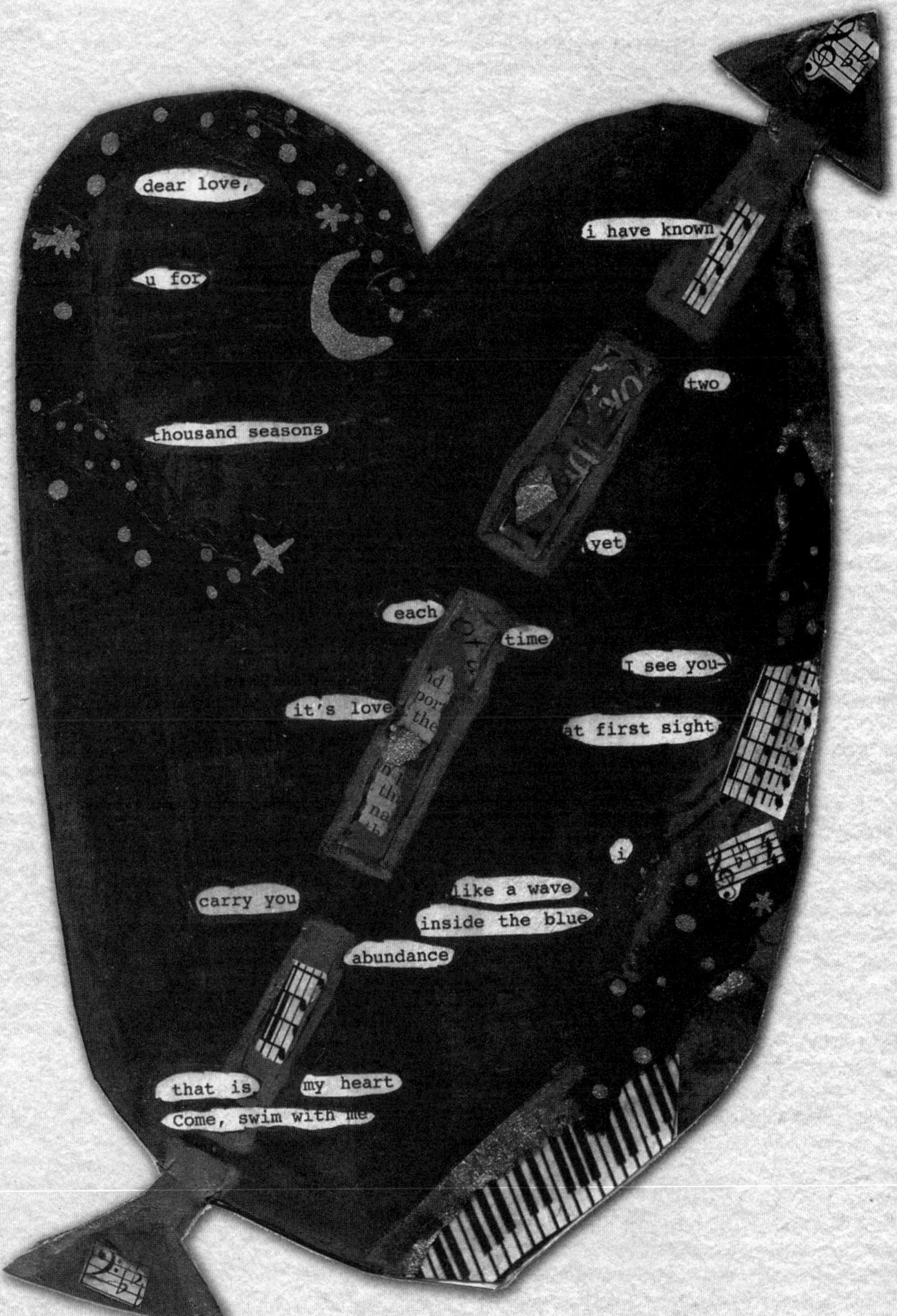
dear love,
u for
thousand seasons
i have known
two
yet
each
time
I see you-
it's love
at first sight
i
carry you
like a wave
inside the blue
abundance
that is
my heart
Come, swim with me.

Heart Attack

Someone snuck it into my bag.
Someone? I ask.

Is Walt pranking me?
. . . .

Noah, is he?
C'mon, Sam, why would he do that? I say, wishing I'd
had the courage to own my cool, despite my fury.

Sounds like something Walt would do. It can't be Cruz.
He's not romantic like this. I mean, he's sorta romantic.
But he's never been romantic this way before. And, do not
tell him about this.
. . . .

Who do you think it might be? She shoots me the look I
can't resist.
It takes every ounce of community theater experience
I've got, which is very little, to act like I've never seen it
before.
I don't know, I respond.

How long is two thousand seasons?
Like a hundred or two hundred years? Have you known
anyone that long?

Stop being silly, Noah. I'm serious. We need to figure this
out. I'm feeling a certain kind of way.
Like bad?

Not bad. Like something else. It feels nice, I guess.
. . . .

Awww . . . you're blushing. I did too, when I first read it.
I'm not blushing, I want to tell her. I'm pissed. I'M

154

PISSED! She pinches my cheek. Why would Walt do
this to me?

So . . .
No idea.

Could be a stalker.
Yeah.

She looks at me. Studies my face.
For a second, I worry

she knows what I know,
that everything isn't copacetic.

Written

all over her face
is a smile

peeking through
the confusion,

a hint
of hope

that this
could be real.

It is, I want to tell her,
just not like this.

Not today. NOT NOW!
What is even realer is

someone's gonna
pay dearly.

Please don't tell anybody about this, Noah.
Okay.

I mean it. Not one person. Promise.
Promise.

Don't lie.
What do you mean?

You know you're gonna tell Walt. Y'all tell each other
everything. You're like old church ladies.
. . . .

But no one else, okay?
I got it, I repeat as she finishes her pizza.

We get up,
and she walks away

on a cloud
of happy.

Truth

Never
    been
a
    violent
person
    but
right
    now
I
    feel
like
    going
to
    batting
practice
    on
Walt's
    head.

I walk

up to him
in the hallway,
but before
I can commence
swinging, he says:

Before you say anything,
I did it
for your own good,
and you even said
it was time
to take
the training wheels off,
and every single word
was true, was it not,
and there should be
a statute
of limitations
on unrequited love.

When Your Best Friend Is Trying to Ruin Your Life

She doesn't know who it's from, so don't worry! There's still time to make this love shine brighter.

. . . .

You think I did this to you? I did it FOR you, homeboy. You needed help. You needed that push.

. . . .

I'm not gonna just let you sit there and watch the world go by, while the girl of your dreams gets swept up in life.

. . . .

That's fine, don't say anything, but I bet it worked. She liked it, didn't she? Trust your indelible words.

. . . .

The train is moving, yo. Time to get on board. Say something, Noah.

. . . .

SHUT THE FREAK UP

is what I want
to yell
at Walt
as he blathers on
about why
he had to do it
on my behalf.

Instead,
I just ignore him.
Walk away.
Get in my car,
turn up the music
on my almost-dead, crackling radio,
and burn rubber,
leaving him
right there
on the school curb.

Stuck

He's right;
the train is rolling,
but I'm not on it.

I'm standing
in the middle
of the track.

Stuck.

My Heart

I wish she'd call.
I want to know

what she's thinking.
I want to know

how she's feeling,
but I'm afraid to dial—

to dial her number,
afraid to text—

afraid that anything
will open up the universe

of this blackout fiasco—
this black hole

of my existence.
What if I get

sucked into
the end

of everything,
and all that's left

are a couple
circled words?

Finally

8:14 pm
Noah, maybe it's Cruz.

8:16 pm
Noah, you there?

8:16 pm
Yup.

8:16 pm
Would be so sweet,
if it's him.

8:19 pm
It's not him.

8:19 pm
How do you know?

8:19 pm
He's not exactly Rimbaud.

8:20 pm
What does that mean?

8:20 pm
Has he ever read a book,
let alone written
something besides

8:20 pm
a baseball scorecard?

8:21 pm
RUDE!

8:21 pm
I'm just saying.

8:21 pm
HATER!!!

8:21 pm
. . . .

8:22 pm
. . . .

8:22 pm
I'm sorry, Sam.
I mean, I guess it could be
Cruz.

8:22 pm
I'll let you know
if I get another one,
okay?

8:24 pm
You want another one?

When Walt strolls

into my house
with a dozen red velvet cupcakes,
interrupting
my train of thought
599 times
to tell me
he's sorry
I wish I'd never
given him
a key.

Apology

I guess I shoulda asked you,
convinced you
it was a genius plan.
But you needed the push, bro.
You weren't gonna
help yourself,
honor your talents.
I'm sorry I didn't
consult with you first.

Shut up.

But it was like waiting
for my little cousin Leroy
to learn to walk
and get off the bottle.
He liked being carried around.
It felt safe.
And I need you
to stop crawling,
stop playing it safe,
and start walking . . .
no, running toward
all the opportunities.

Shut up.

You have to grow, bro.
Take a chance.
If I didn't act fast
for you,
you'd still be
secretly scribbling hearts
with Sam's name on it
for the next eighty years.

I guess I was wrong,
and for that
I'm immensely sorry.
Maybe you just
need to fail
without even trying.
It's your life,
and you gotta do
what you gotta do,
learn the way you
need to learn,
live the way
you wanna live.

PLEASE, SHUT UP!

Noise

But it's difficult, man.
I love you like a brother,
and I want to see you
dare to enter
the cave of uncertainty,
find your way out
to the other side,
where the light
of reward awaits.
You feel me?
You understand me?
You forgive me?
Dude, where ya going?

I slam my door

loud enough
for the house to rattle,
and for Walt to get
the point.

Still, I wish
I'd taken
the cupcakes.

The Price of Betrayal

It's been a weekend
of dreary weather
inside
and out,
of Walt walking around
like a ghost.
I haven't spoken
one word to him,
not one.
Not even to tell him
to knock it off
when he slurps
his SpaghettiOs
or cereal loudly
in the next room.

I lock myself inside
my four walls,
even though I know
it's killing him
that I'm not acknowledging
he's here.

I'm not ready to accept
his pathetic apology.
Even if most
of what he says
makes sense,
it doesn't take away
from the fact
he stole
my art like a thief,
gave it to Sam,
risking my humiliation.

She wasn't supposed
to see
my drawings.
It's not something
I ever planned to share.
It's a piece of me
that should
stay hidden
inside the History
of the Unseen.

If this ruins my chances
with Sam,
I don't know how
or if
I'll ever
forgive him.

Starbucks

Where's Swing?
I don't know, Sam.

Uh, isn't he staying at your place?
My guess is he's on his way.

Where?
Here.

Why didn't he ride with you?
Because.

I don't understand.
Look, I'm not in charge of Walt's whereabouts.

Trouble in paradise. You guys have a tiff?
He pissed me off, yeah!

What happened?
Nothing I want to talk about, actually.

. . . .

. . . .

Fine, I'll change the subject. Are you guys really having a party?
I don't know—I'm not really feeling it.

It's not the worst idea. I can ask Cruz to get his older brother to bring some beer.
I don't drink beer.

Not for us, for everybody else, so your party's not lame.

. . . .

Geesh, who spit in your cereal? Coffee's taking forever this morning.

. . . .

By the way, in case you were worried, there's no need.
I'm safe.
Huh?

The heart-shaped letter thingy from X, my anonymous
suitor. I didn't get another one.
Well, at least no one's stalking you. That's good.

I guess.
What do you mean?

I was kinda hoping I did have a secret admirer.
Oh.

Oh well. At least I've got Cruz. You coming to his game
with me?
I'm having dinner with my granny, I lie, knowing
I don't want
to go and watch
Sam's boyfriend
knock another ball
out the park.

On Tuesday

I'm eating onion rings
and leftover
mac and cheese
when the doorbell buzzes
like five times in a row.

I walk over
to the front door,
look through
the tiny peephole,
but don't see anyone
standing on the porch.

I swing the door open,
thinking I'm about to
bust one of the
neighborhood kids
ding-dong ditching me,
and all I see
is the biggest bag
of party ice
on my front steps.

A bag of ice?
I'm confused
and a little worried
what this prank
might mean,
or if it's an ominous
message from Cruz.

Then I look out
into the yard
and see Walt
practically standing

in the azaleas,
with his Hug Life arms
holding
an enormous sign
above his head
that says:
LET'S BREAK THE ICE.

I can't help but laugh
at Walt's ridiculousness,
at how crazy he looks,
at how clever he is,
and at the fact
that even though
he annoys
the heck out of me
and drives me insane,
he is my very best friend.

I shake my head,
walk away,
go back inside,
leaving the front door
wide open

for Walt.

Apology Accepted

So, we good?

. . . .

You want to talk about it?
Nope.

If your brother pisses you off, tell him about it. If he listens to you, he is your brother for life.
Real profound.

It is. Matthew said it.
Who's Matthew?

The Bible Matthew, yo!
I doubt the Bible says pissed off, Walt.

I was paraphrasing. Just trying to elucidate the power of communication between brothers.

. . . .

Did she like your heart?
She liked the heart.

Did she love the heart?

. . . .

SHE. LOVED. THE. HEART, DIDN'T SHE?! I KNEW IT. *My plan worked.*
Don't piss me off again.

You should do another one, if she liked it that much.

. . . .

Seriously, you could woo her like Steve Martin.
What are you talking about?

Roxanne!
Who's Roxanne?

Daryl Hannah played Roxanne in a movie with Steve Martin, who wrote her love letters for a friend of his. It's like Cyrano.
Oh!

Cyrano de Bergerac.
Yeah, I know. How'd he die?

Nobody's really sure, but he was either injured by a wooden beam, a botched assassination attempt, or he went insane and stabbed himself, and—
BAM! Yeah, I get it.

Are we cool, bro?
Yeah.

Come on, let's hug it out. HUG life, Noah.
Do we have to?

Yo, I'm hungry.
Me too.

Let's go grab a burrito.
Sure, but promise me you won't crumble up nacho chips and put them inside.

I cannot make that promise.
. . . .

On the way, I need to make a stop.
Where?

The Baddest Girl on Earth

She has long, jet-black hair,
eyes the color of dark amber
framed in hot-nerd, black-rimmed glasses.

There's something enchanting about her.
I want to watch the rhythm
in her walk,

hear the lilt in
her raspy voice,
look into her eyes

and see her story
from beginning to now.
I've gotta see her again, Noah.

So, we go back

to the thrift store
'cause Walt
wants to see the girl
who rocks his world,
and he needs me
to be
his wingman
in case
I get nervous
and can't actually speak.

In case? Ha!

Conversation

You're back. Did your mom like the bag?
She loved it, I say, wondering if I should tell her about
the letters we found.

Hey, Swing, she says to Walt, who's indeed unable to get
words out of his mouth, so he waves. *What can I help you
two with this time?*
I'm having a party.

Wicked!
And I guess I need to buy some good music for that party.

You ever heard of streaming?
I'm old-fashioned, I lie. Got records?

Plenty. What kind of music?
I find that the tonality of jazz on vinyl really inhabits you,
Walt says, finally acting as if he's alive.

Oh really, she says.
Take, for instance, Miles Davis, he continues, his
confidence building, his awkwardness fading. *Kind of
Blue is a classic example.*

Actually, it's not, Divya counters.
Huh? Walt says, frowning.

*Abandoning the traditional major and minor key
relationships of tonality, Miles based the entire album on
modality. It was a remarkable, landmark album that shaped
the future of modern music. It was improvisation, but each
of the performers was given a set of scales that defined the
parameters of their improvisation.*
Well, I guess there's a new sheriff in town, I say, laughing
a little.

Uh, Walt utters, almost speechless again.

Nonetheless, jazz at a high school house party sounds like my kind of party. That's rad, fellas.

You should come, I say to her, 'cause Walt's not speaking again, even though his mouth is wide open. As is his nose.
Maybe I will. Here's the jazz section. You want vocals or instrumental? Ella or John Coltrane—

July 17, 1967. Coltrane died from a tumor on his liver, Walt says, getting his bearings back. *Had a weight problem, got real fat, fell over on his porch on Staten Island, and three weeks later, BAM!*
Actually, it was Long Island.

I think I'm in love, Walt says, looking directly at her, not realizing that he actually says it out loud.

Birth of the Cool

I watch Walt stare
at Divya
like a loyal puppy
while she plays
different songs
on a vintage record player
and he guesses
who's playing.

You're good, Swing, she says to him, after he tells her the
name of record number five.
"Salt Peanuts." *That's bebop and scat. Dizzy Gillespie,
baby!*

Okay, last one, for the win, she says as she puts the needle
on the record.
. . . .

Well, Divya says, *I'll need an answer.
Is it . . . Dexter Gordon?*

*You're getting warm.
Charlie Parker?*

*Cold.
Give me a hint.*

*Miles Davis.
I didn't say tell me who it is.*

What's the tune, then?
. . . .

*It's named after one of the most famous ancient Greek
sculptures.*
. . . .

Venus de Milo, I say.
SCORE for Noah, Divya says, holding my hands up.
Ladies and gents, we have a new grand champion.

Not fair. I thought this was jazz trivia, not art.
It's all related, Mr. Swing.

It's actually a misnomer. The sculpture should have been called—
Aphrodite of Milos, Divya interrupts.

Because Venus is the Roman goddess of love, and Aphrodite is the Greek goddess, I finish.
Wow, Noah, you know your art.

I dabble. Plus, she's beautiful and confident and assured and full of passion.
So, you've been to the Louvre?

No.
Then how'd you see her?

In a book.
You gotta see it in person. It's breathtaking.

Have you been to the Louvre?
When I was nine, we went to Paris. I remember like it was yesterday. The Mona Lisa is also there. Art can really inspire you to embrace the preciousness of life.

Agree completely.
Can we get back to jazz, please, Walt says, looking a little irritated.

Here, she says, handing him the Miles Davis album, *this is for you, my treat. It's one of my faves. Could be your autobiography too, Mr. Swing*, she says, winking at him.

An hour later

we leave
with her phone number
written
on the sweaty palm
of his left hand,
and three jazz albums,
including
the one he keeps
staring at,
the one
she gave him:
Birth of the Cool.

The Only Thing That Can Shut Walt Up

We don't talk about
the flags
we see in yards
and on windshields
of parked cars.

We don't talk about
the three-legged dog
that runs
into the street,
almost getting hit.

We don't talk about
the English paper
due tomorrow
at 9:00 in the morning.

We don't talk about
dead celebs
or any of Walt's obsessions.

We don't even talk about
his brother's return, or
his mom's impending wedding.

In fact, we don't talk
about anything at all,
because Walt is out of his mind
over a goddess
who is way smarter
and way older
than he is.

Out of His Mind

DOPAMINE!
Huh?

Dopamine.
What are you talking about, Walt?

I'm gonna marry her.
Dude, you just met her.

*It only takes between ninety seconds and four minutes
to decide if you're into someone. We call it love, but it's
really just the chemical dopamine. It stimulates desire and
reward by triggering an intense rush of pleasure. It has
the same effect on the brain as taking cocaine. I'm high on
Divya Konar, Noah!*
You're high on something.

*She's coming to the party. Which means we've got work to
do. Need to make it the best party ever. For both of us!*
So, we're definitely gonna stick with the whole jazz-
music-at-a-house party?

*Yeah, I'm gonna ask my Uncle Stanley Stanley to bring his
trio.*
He's got two first names.

*Yep, but don't mention it—he's real sensitive about his
names.*
I don't know about this.

Go bold or go home.
Go home.

So, you're down with it?
Do I have a choice?

186

When we get home

I FaceTime
Mom
and Dad
while Walt climbs to
the attic
looking for
a turntable
I don't even think
we have.

I FOUND IT, he screams from the attic, and
for the next three hours,
we listen
to the same record
over and over.

And over.

134 minutes
of another street,
another town,
a different country,
a newfound planet.
A place where
jazz is king,
where the mind is all lit,
and what Swing calls
a transcendence of sorts.
And I do kinda feel it,
like maybe the rhythm
gets me.

So, I draw.

You hear cool, Noah?

I hear way past cool, Walt.
I hear watermelon
on a summer night.

I hear
the sound
of a million stars
singing
of pristine love.

I hear a trumpet
serenading
lovers.

Corinthian and
Annemarie dancing
to an endless groove.

You hear all that, Noah?
Yeah, and I hear her.

Who?
Sam.

Yeah?
Yeah,
and I want to dive into
her smile, swim
from one corner
of her mouth
to the other.

Really?
Really.

. . . .
What do you think? I ask, showing him my drawing.

Dope.
I'm doing it, I say, feeling confident.

Doing what?
I'm gonna give it to her.

Part 3

Second Balcony Jump

Guess Who?

Sam comes up to me
at my locker.
I got another one, she says,
grinning with wonder
like it's Christmas morning.

She tells me
who she thinks
her anonymous
secret admirer
is, but
none of her guesses
are me,
which is a relief
and a disappointment.

Conversation

It's gorgeous. And thoughtful. And, whoever is doing this is smart and sexy.
That eliminates ninety percent of the guys in this school.

Maybe it's a girl.
Maybe.

Whoever it is has me all up in my feelings.
Yeah?

Noah, I feel like a flower blossoming, and these letters are my sunshine.

. . . .

You want to see it?
Sure, I say, smiling confidently, as if I didn't draw it last night.

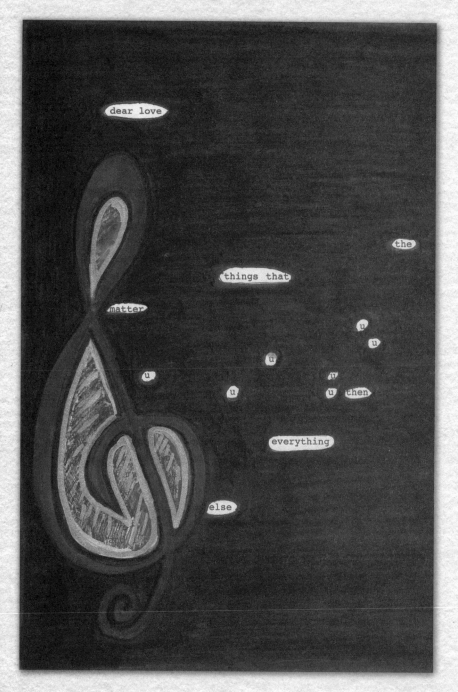

Close, But No Cigar

I gave it to her.
And?

And she loved it.
So, the cat's out of the bag?

Not exactly.
That sounds suspicious, bro.

Let's say the cat's peeking.
. . . .

I gave it to her, but haven't told her it's me yet. One step
at a time.
I know just what you need.

I hope it's not Dairy Queen.
Ha!

Primer Three

Listen to this, Noah, he says, streaming
more jazz
from his phone.
Jazz is
an unpredictable friend,
full of love and rage,
whimsy and woe.
It's fire and ice.
It's all that, huh? I say, with a little sarcasm.

Feel it, Noah.
Live inside the rhythm.
Follow the pulse.
To win over Sam's heart,
you gotta become
fire and ice,
like jazz!
Huh?

Tell me what you hear!

I hear

giant steps
across pavement,
running for life
in New York City
or Chicago,
or some big city,
bolting
down a street,
trying to get away
from evil.

Escaping
down an alleyway
or a crowded street,
into a hotel lobby,
where a beautiful girl
walks in
with all the confidence
in the world.

Good! Okay, what else, Noah?

The girl grabs my hand,
we both run
in the opposite direction
from where I came.
We keep running
until we're almost out of breath,
hoping we're safe, free.

Then, we fall, exhausted,
our hearts pounding
to the point of explosion,
but evil returns
and I'm forced

to fight,
to try
and save her.

Yo, this is crazy stuff, Swing!
I got a headache.
But was it a good run.
I guess. So was I close? What's the tune about?

No idea—it's a Charles Mingus tune called "All the Things You Could Be by Now If Sigmund Freud's Wife was Your Mother."
Seriously, Sigmund Freud, the shrink? Bananas! Hey, how'd he die?

Mingus died of ALS, on a Friday. Seems like a lot of jazz musicians die on Fridays.
No, Freud. How'd he die?

Morphine overdose.
He killed himself?

Basically, yeah. But he had a doctor friend actually administer it.
That's crazy. Pun intended.

It was a Saturday. September 23, 1939. Same day the Dodgers beat the Phillies 22–4. I bet that was a good game. Hey, I'm sure there's a game on. Let's get some popcorn and study the plays.
I'm studying my eyelids, yo. Good night.

Starbucks Fix No. 1,299

I drop Walt off
and park the car
in the lot
across the street.

Seems the whole student body
is in here.
Everybody needs
their midterm fix.

When I get inside,
Walt's talking to—Wait, why is he
talking to Cruz?
Why are they laughing?
What are they laughing about?
I try to pretend like
I don't see them,
but Walt waves me over
before I can look
away.

Never Mix the Wrong Drinks and the Wrong Company

We're waiting for Walt's
ridiculous chai latte
sprinkled
with mocha caramel
and elderberry syrup
when Cruz says,
I need your advice, Noah,
then chugs
an energy drink
like a muscle-bound
walking cliché.

Awkward Conversation with Cruz

You need my advice?
Well, both of you. Whoever, he says, motioning his fingers
to pull us in closer.

What do you need? Walt asks.
How do I close the deal with Sam—really close the deal?

Close what deal? I ask with a lump in my throat, because
I think I know what he means.
*You know what I mean. It's home run time. Should I buy
her flowers, bring her chocolate, sing her a song, make her
a playlist, play with her hair?*

Filet-O-Fish and fries, she'll love that, I say, knowing
she'll hate it, because she hasn't eaten McDonald's since
fourth grade, when she found a fly in her fries.
Really, Cruz says. *You think so?*

Women are hard to figure out, Walt adds, winking at me.
No rhyme or reason.
True. Well, it's going down tonight.
Walt and I stand there
for what seems like
an awkward forever,
staring silently
into the haze
of a caffeine fog
with Cruz,
until we're saved
by the barista,
who screams
out—

BLACK LIVES MATTER!

Last time I was here, I told them my name was Barry Bonds,
Walt says, smiling and collecting his coffee mashup.
Time before that it was Voldemort or Dump Trump, I can't
remember. Just depends on how I feel that day.
So, you're feeling like Colin Kaepernick?

Noah, the struggle is real out here in these mean streets.
Walt, you live in a gated community.

We are all part of America. United in our values, in
our belief that basic respect of life and humanity is a
prerequisite for true democracy.
You're running for the office of president now?

I'm running for the office of black boys are being killed and
nobody seems to care.
. . . .

Anyway, enough of that, he says once Cruz is out of
earshot. *You better watch out.*
For what?

Noah, Cruz is playing hardball.
. . . .

The window to your happiness is closing.
I'm working on another love note, I say, handing him my
latest.

dear love,

                              i want to
                         lift u
                         like a
          window   Climb inside yr
                    pane,

     chase   u like
                                 a squirrel

     through harlem.

Squirrels and Lovers

What in the world is this?
What are you talkin' about?

I don't remember seeing anything about squirrels in Corinthian's letters.

It's a mashup. I mean, it was a magazine article I found. I'm doing what Floyd said to do. Painting her my own world. Crashing through the door of my own destiny.

I hear ya, but you're gonna chase her like a squirrel through Harlem? C'mon, yo!
Well, it sounded romantic.

You just half-colored the page black and weren't intentional with design or even the words.
That's why it's called a draft. I'm still working on it.

This is trash.
Why don't you say how you really feel?

It's a disgrace to Corinthian.
You know how difficult these pieces are? Art takes time.

You can't give her this.
I said I'm worki—

You can't give her any iteration of this. I say start over.
You wanna help?

You're the artist.
C'mon, man.

Can't! Got a date.
Seriously?

Well, it's a phone date. Divya and I are scheduled to talk in exactly, he says, *ten minutes, and I need to practice.*
Practice?

Because I suck at phone conversations. If I can't see the person, I find it horribly unsettling to actually say stuff to them. And I end up talking too loud.

It's who you are, Swing. Be you. That's what you would tell me.

Disgusting

I stay up
'til three am
composing
and cutting
and pasting,
and the next morning
when I come downstairs,
Walt has cooked breakfast,
which is great
'cause I'm starving,
and I love
scrambled eggs,
grits, and
turkey sausage,
but it's also not so great
'cause now
I gotta watch him
mix it all together
in a bowl and
eat it.

Conversation with Walt

Breakfast smells good.
*You look terrible, man. Did you stay up all night reworking
that horrid piece of art?*

Yeah, but I couldn't figure it out. That's art sometimes.
That's life sometimes.

Can you turn the music down a tad? I'm still waking up.
The wave is coming, Noah!

Huh?
That's the song playing—"Wave"! Amazing, isn't it?

Hmmm. I wouldn't call it amazing, but it's decent.
Decent? Yo, this is quintessential bossa nova.

. . . .

It's Brazilian jazz.

Oh. It kinda sounds like I'm on an elevator going up to
my dreaded dentist appointment.
*I don't know what elevator you've been riding on, but this
is pure magic. THIS is what floating inside a love boat on
the serene sea of soulmates feels like.*

A love boat, dude . . . soulmates? What is going on? Are
you in . . .
Love? I could be. Divya likes me, man.

Congratulations.
*She really likes me. She laughed like a songbird at my
brilliant wit, and her velvety violin of a voice soothed my
nerves as soon as we got on the phone. I think it went
really, really well. My first phone date . . .*

Your first date, period.
*We made a connection. And that's what's important. Looks
like one of us had a successful night.*

Whatever.
So back to your art . . .

Yeah, I don't know. Maybe I do suck.
*You know what you need to do. You need to listen to the
song. Really listen to it. Again. And again. So, close your
eyes and tap into the rhythm of the song. Escape into it,
float away on the—*

Wave, yeah, I get it already, I say, not ready
to admit that
the rhythmic guitar
and the smooth piano
and the soft drums
and, yeah,
the waves,
are kinda refreshing.

Searching

I look for Sam
all over
school,
but she's not in any
of her usual spots.
I reluctantly
walk up
to Cruz,
who's standing
in the hallway
with his baseball buddies.
Hey, Cruz, do you know where Sam is?
He shrugs
his shoulder,
winches
his face
like he doesn't know
and doesn't care,
then turns his back
and starts talking
and laughing
like I was never
even there.

MIA

Sam is nowhere to be seen.
Walt doesn't know.
She's not in class.
Not in the usual hallways.
Not in the cafeteria.
Not outside her locker.
Not in school.
Vanished.
Maybe she knows.
Maybe she got my latest
and she hates it.

Maybe she hates me.

Text to Sam

2:12 pm
Sam, are you okay?
Walt and I are worried. Please
holla back ASAP.

Text from Sam

5:37 pm
NOAH, CALL ME! IT'S
AN EMERGENCY. I CAN'T
BELIEVE THIS HAPPENED!

What Happened Was

You okay, Sam?
No. I hate Cruz, she says, between tears.

What happened? What did he do?
*He said we were going on a date and he took me to
McDonalds, which I told him I hated—and how could
he not know that after we've been going out for this long?
Then he called me stuck up, and we started arguing right
there in the middle of McDonalds. Then he said he needed
a break.*

A break?
He broke up with me.

. . . .

I told him things were moving too fast.

. . . .

Then he kirked off, said I was teasing him along.

I'm sorry, Sam.
I just hate him, she says, still sobbing.

You want me to come over?
I want ice cream.

I can bring you some.
Meet me at Dairy Queen. One hour.

How about I bring you Breyers?
That's fine. Just hurry.

I throw my clothes on

quicker than Clark Kent
turning into Superman,
run downstairs,
see Walt
passed out
with smooth jazz
as his lullaby.
I grab my car keys,
quietly head out
the door
for my date
with ice cream
and destiny.

Mayhem

On my way
into the convenience store
to get ice cream
for Sam,
a police officer stops me,
starts asking
if I saw anything.

A UPS truck driver
comes by, says,
He was a white guy,
big and scary-looking,
with a lot of hair, but
he was short
and he ran fast,
though he could have been
black, but I think
he was white.

An older woman
is crying,
pointing to
her groceries
on the ground.
He was tall
and scary, like
a giant, and he
knocked over
my bag,
but he stopped
and started helping me
pick everything up. Then
we heard sirens
and he ran away.

YEAH, I SAW HIM,
I SAW HIM,
a man in glasses
says frantically
to the police officers.
HE WAS TALL, MAYBE
BROWN, MAYBE TAN
IN THE FACE, AND HE
LOOKED LIKE HIM,
he continues,
pointing to the UPS driver,
and getting angry
'cause the police
won't let him remove
the dozen
or so
miniature flags
behind the wipers
on his car windshield.
Calm down, one of the officers says.
He was putting the flags on my car,
and he was screaming.
I don't know who
he was screaming at,
but when he saw me,
he ran. He ran fast,
like his feet were
on fire.

Did you see anything? one
of the officers
asks me.
No, sir, I say, tasting the sweat
dripping down

my face.
I just got here.

He went that way, says a raspy voice I recognize.

I turn around
to see the old man
with the trumpet
pointing to the sky.
*He flew, like a bird in the clouds. Couldn't even get a good
look at him,* he continues,
then disappears
into the store
as quickly
as he appeared.

Chance Encounter

I head into the store,
anxious
and hot,
to the freezer section
for ice cream
for Sam.
I open a door
and stick my head in
to cool off.

I grab the one
that's on sale,
and as I turn the corner
to go pay,
there he is,
almost like
he's waiting
for me.

There's something
about this man
and his trumpet.
Here one minute,
gone the next,
then back again
like a ghost,
or an angel.

It's you, I say.
It is I.

Phantom

You okay, Youngblood? You look ruffled, he says, like he
actually cares.
It's just everything's kinda outta control right now.
Everyone's freakin' out about those flags, and then I
see you again, and I think you said something about
somebody flying. And on top of it, my best friend, this girl
I've cared about for years, got her heart ripped out by her
boyfriend, so I'm bringing her ice cream to cheer her up.

*You're worried about people flying. I'm worried that you're
bringing your friend ice cream to cure a broken heart.
That's just empty calories.*
Yeah, I know, but she loves ice cream. We used to eat
frozen yogurt and ice cream together all the time. To
celebrate birthdays and good grades.

You love her.
Huh? She's my friend.

You love her more than a friend, he says, laughing with his
few teeth and gums showing.
. . . .

*It's in your walk. Shoot, man, the desperation in your eyes is
blinding. Let me put my shades back on.*
. . . .

*A little advice. Ice cream will only cool her down and freeze
her tongue. You want to put fire in her heart, bring her
something that fills her with warmth.*
What, like hot sauce?

He laughs so hard,
the cashier asks us
to hurry up,
if we're buying something.

220

Youngblood, a life without the warmth of love is a sunless
garden when the flowers are dead.
Huh?

Follow me, he gestures, and
we walk
to the floral section.

What do you suppose she'd like?
Flower-wise? I point to some red puffball-looking things.

Carnations are the cheap man's rose.
Perfect, I say, grabbing a handful.

Stop, son. Put those down. Is she a name for you to post,
a picture for you to share? Or is she the flowering garden
that will bloom over and over again, with an abundance of
possibilities?
The garden, I guess.

You guess? What is she to you?
One of my best friends. The only girl I ever dream about,
ever think about.

The rarest of sapphires?
Yeah, I guess.

. . . .

I mean, yes, she is, most definitely.

Give her a blue orchid. Tell her it is rare, stunning, and
strong like her. It will last as long as she nurtures it. And it
will bloom again. Just like she will.
You haven't even seen her.

No, but the way you were running through the store to
grab a pint of ice cream for a girl, I knew.
Doesn't look like they have orchids.

Then pick something else, something electric, he says,

walking up the aisle
and out
of the store,
whistling something
I think Walt has
played for me
before.

I pick up
the most electric flowers
on sale
and jet.

Happiness

Who died?
Huh?

The flowers.
They're for you, Sam.

They're gladiolus. Funeral flowers, Noah.
Oh, my bad. I thought they looked pretty, I guess.

The thought is what matters.
Well, you can't go wrong with ice cream.

*Awww, you're so sweet. You're the only one who listens to
me, who really knows me.*
. . . .

You want a cone too?
Sure.

We sit at her kitchen counter,
and she devours her scoop
like she's starved
with sadness.
Her eyes say
her soul
is wandering
or lost.
I know I need to find a way
to make her feel good
again.

Want to talk about it? I ask.
Not really.

You deserve . . .
Better. Yeah, I know.

Yeah . . . Well, it's true.
Come with me to the living room. There's something I want to do.

Trap

Come, sit down.
She leads me to the couch
like a psychiatrist
prepping a patient
for a mental evaluation.

Love and ice cream are all we really need, Noah.
True.

Oh, I almost forgot, I got another love letter, she says,
reaching into her backpack.
. . . .

*It was in the mailbox. If I hadn't come home early, my
mom would have checked the box and asked me like a
hundred questions.*
. . . .

It's the one bright spot in all this darkness.
. . . .

*Here, look. Help me read between the lines to figure out
who this rebel is, okay?*
She shuffles them around
as I try to think
of an exit plan,
because I can feel a panic
swell up in me,
but I don't want to be
a wimp.

*They're all so random, romantic, intelligent. Who is this X,
Noah?*
No idea.

Let's read them aloud. It'll be like theater class last year.

225

I got a C minus in that class. Remember? I think it's better if you just read them.

Come on, Noah. It would make me smile.
Fine.

Love Is the Reader

She hands me
the first one,
the one Walt stole and delivered,
the one that started this whole thing.
And for a moment in my mind,
I am pummeling him.
But her wide grin softens me.
Go ahead, Noah. Read.

So, I read.

Awww, you're blushing again!
Am not. I'm just hot, I lie.

I look down,
continue reading
the most recent one,
trying not to suffocate,
trying not to melt.
I just want to escape
the fire
as fast
as possible.

I finish
as a trickle of sweat
drips down
onto the paper.

*I think you should have gotten an A in theater class. You
read like a pro. You read like a boy who knows love.*
. . . .

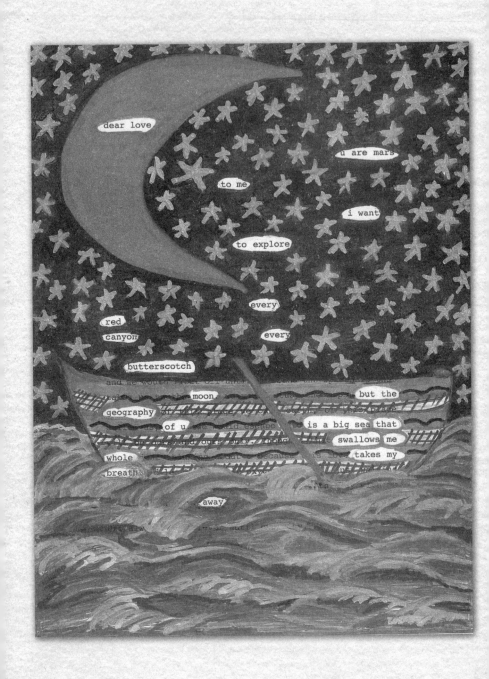

X-Man

There is a sign
in the front yard
of my heart, she says,
after we are both silent
for long enough.

It reads: No trespassing.
But now, this:
A secret
painted on the wall
of my desire.

Noah, I must tell you,
I don't want to play
the game
of love anymore.

Cruz has spoiled
everything
for me.

But X gives me hope.
Who are you?
Who is he, Noah?

No Dice

We lie next to each other,
sink into her old couch,
feeding each other
more mint chocolate chip
like we were meant
to be.

My heart, a steel drum.
It pounds. POUNDS!
Should I kiss her?
I've never kissed anyone.
I put my arm around her,
try to comfort her.
She inches closer.
My arm feels like
it's going to dislodge
from my shoulder
and float away
in bliss.
Her hair
smells like fresh sea.
I close my eyes.
The Wave is on its way.
I hear Walt:
Go for it, bro. You have to take these chances while you
have them.
And as I move
my head closer to hers,
she says,
You know, Noah, I'm feeling better. You're like the sweetest
brother a girl could ever have.

And just like that,
all my dreams
come true
are blown.

A Secret

Her phone rings.
Over and over.
I'm not talking to him, she says, throwing the phone
across the room.

She turns off
the TV,
sits up,
grabs my hand.

You still having your party?
Walt's been doing all the planning, so yeah, I guess. You
still coming?

I don't know.
. . . .

Did I ever tell you why my parents got divorced?
No, you didn't. And I felt bad asking . . . and that's why I
never . . . She squeezes my hand. Hard.

*Well, five years ago, our German shepherd Lucy ate some
woman's lingerie. When they recovered the skimpy outfit
from Lucy's gut, things got a little awkward when Mom
realized the vet tech wasn't holding up her lingerie.*
Dang.

*Yeah. It's an embarrassing story. But I'm starting to wonder
if I'll ever trust another guy because of it.*
Not all men are like that, Sam. Not my dad, not me.

No, I know. It's only the jerks who like me and my mom.
Things happen, and sometimes people pick the wrong
people.

*Maybe. Don't ever tell anyone what I just told you, Noah.
Promise.*

I promise.

You don't have any secrets, Noah. Never have. You're a
perfectly normal guy.

. . . .

King of Heartbreaks

As I'm leaving,
her phone rings.
Again.

Cruz.

It's definitely him calling.
We both stare
at the phone,
at each other,
at nothing
and everything.

Please, don't answer, I think.
He probably wants her back.
Please, don't answer.
I see a sparkle of hope in her eyes,
the feeling you get
when there's snow
on the ground
and you get an alert
that school is cancelled.
The promise of possibility.
She's going to answer.
She's. Going. To. Answer.
Run back
into his suffocating arms,
and I'll be eating
ice cream by myself.

Please, don't answer.

Text to Swing

5:32 pm
Swing, I'm leaving Sam's house.
Wanna hang?
Where are you?

Text from Swing

5:39 pm
The batting cage.
Come watch the magic, bro.
Baby Bonds is a machine.

Ceiling lights

beam down
on Walt,
and—Wait, what's he doing here?

Yo, Noah!
Hey . . . Floyd.

In between
Walt's mostly missed
few hits,
Floyd pitches
a string
of curveball metaphors.

The Metaphors

You've got to use your love muscle or it loses strength . . .
Muscle has memory, just like your brain . . . Your heart
is your greatest muscle. Without it, you miss the ball . . .
You gotta reset . . . You need to think about what's in
your head and what's getting in the way of the big hit . . .
Relationships are the same way . . . If you strike out, you're
just plain doin' something wrong. You're not taking this
thing seriously . . . A bat is like cupid's arrow . . . You only
have so many chances before you strike out . . . Ya know,
a fly ball is like a relationship; once it catches air, your
chances for a home run are pretty good . . . But, you can't
miss her signal. If you do, you need to reset. It's up to you
to hit the ball and run to first, slide into all the bases . . .
You keep striking out, you need to stop and think, what am
I doing wrong?
What am I doing wrong, Floyd? I ask.

Out of two hundred balls

Walt hits forty.
He's getting better
at the stance,
at the swing,
at the hit;
and either Floyd's metaphors
are getting less worse
by the minute
or I'm starting
to understand
and believe his guru-ish.

Floyd heard what you're doing, bro.
Doing? What do you mean? I ask him.

He's talking about your anonymous art thingies, Walt
chimes in.
You told him?

He's just looking out for you, bro. It's all good.
You suck, Walt, I say, as he smacks a pitch real good, to
his surprise. And mine.

Have you been listening to The Woohoo Woman?
I tried to tell him to, Floyd.

Shut up, Walt. I've been listening. In general.
*But you're lying. And when you're lying, you're not
listening.*

I'm not lying. I took your advice and wrote her.
*The art of the secret love letter is smooth. Floyd gives you
an A plus for ingenuity and delivery, but an F minus for
execution.*

What? Why? She loves them.

Have you told her it's you yet?

Not exactly.
He hasn't, Floyd.

*What's the point in winning her heart if she can't hold
yours in it?*
. . . .

*It's time to write your own life. Let her get to know the real
Noah and how he truly feels.*
I agree, Walt says.

Floyd gets up
in my face,
so close,
I can tell
he doesn't floss.
Then he shoves
his hand
into
my pants pocket.
I squirm.

Dude, what are you doing?
*Showing you the signal, making sure you don't strike out.
Write your life, Noah. Bring X to life,* he says, grabbing
my car keys.

Let her know who you really are at heart, he says,
pounding his heart with one hand and dangling my car
keys with the other. *You can have these back when Floyd
sees you're really trying. Walt, you'll report back to me?
Sure thing, cuz!*

Floyd, come on, man. How are we supposed to get home?
*Come to Dairy Queen for your ride when the mission is
complete.*

239

Walt grabs his bat and glove, and follows his cousin.
Hey, where are you going?

I'm already on base. I got a girl. I'm riding with coach, he
says, dapping Floyd, and
following him
to my car.

Spur of the Moment

On the walk home,
while I daydream
of Sam,
I pass by
Out with the Old
and decide
to stop in.

Thrifting and Riffing

The door dings,
and Divya pops up
from behind the counter
with paper towels
and Windex.

Hey, you.
Hey.

Shopping alone today?
I guess you can say that.

Anything special you're looking for?
Inspiration.

She laughs,
adjusts her glasses.

Well, make it fast, 'cause I close at nine.
I need something that'll make me move.

Move?
As in forward. Reach beyond myself, dig deep. I need to
go, Divya. Like really GO!

You need some Dexter.
I'm not sure becoming a serial killer is the answer.

No, silly, not that Dexter. Dexter Gordon. Best music ever,
she says, walking over to the old record section. *This is
the only one we have of his, but it's pure, unadulterated
jazz genius. Inspiration on so many levels.*
You and Walt are obsessed with jazz.

Great minds think alike, she says, handing me a Dexter
album called *GO!*
Wait, that's actually the name of it, GO? Dang, you're
good.

It was his favorite album. Full of grace, pleasure, and confidence. Listen to it; it'll make you wanna get up and GO!

How much is it?

Your money's no good here. It's on the house. Consider it a thank you.

For what?

For introducing me to Swing.

You know no one seriously calls him that but you.

It's kinda cute. He asked me out on a date. Should I go?

As long as he doesn't take you to the batting cages.

He's there a lot. Pretty committed.

Delusional too. You should go out with him.

I'm thinking about it. I sort of like him. He's not a crazy guy, is he?

Over-the-top crazy, but the coolest guy I know. Unique, one-of-a-kind, you'll-never-meet-anyone-like-him kind of crazy.

I can dig that.

Thanks for the record.

GO get 'em, Noah.

Ha.

When I get home

sitting
on my front porch,
with his eyes closed
and music blasting
from my Bluetooth speaker,
is my best friend.

What are you doing?
Meditating, he says, with his eyes still closed.

Sitting
in the driveway
is my jalopy.

How'd you get the truck back?
I vouched for you, plus he was just funnin'.

Thanks, I say, grabbing the keys.
What took you so long? It's getting chilly.

Had to make a stop.
At Sam's?

The thrift shop, I say, and let it just hang
in the air
for a minute. Divya says hi, I add, walking
into the house.

What else did she say?

Anything about me? he asks.
No, I lie.

Really?
Just kidding.

She said she thinks you're cute.
She said you're more mature than most guys your age.
She said she's going to see her family in India this
summer.
She said Billie Holiday's voice is divine.
She said Herbie Hancock is good, but he's no Erroll
Garner.
She said she hopes you're not a stalker.
She said she was just joking.

Anything else?
Yeah, then she gave me this album, I say, showing off
my gift.

We listen

like we're in church, on
bended knee, and our god
is Dexter Gordon.

Primer Four

GO! is a roller
coaster of emotions, a
carousel of cool,

twisting and turning,
going up and up and up,
so fast, so far, it

shoots me like a
cannonball, and when it comes
down, I am in need

of a parachute
to brace my fall after getting
so high off this groove.

Speechless

I have no words at this moment.
What do you mean?

Ask Yo Mama!
Ask yours.

No, Langston Hughes.
Deciphering your riddles is exhausting.

*Ask Yo Mama is the name of an epic breakdown of jazz
that Langston Hughes wrote.*
Oh.

*You get it. You. Finally. Get. Jazz. The student has become
the master.*
It's a good album.

It's a great album.
By the way, I say on my way up the stairs to my room,
Sam and Cruz broke up.

*WHAT?! Dude, you should have led with that. Tell me
what happened.*
Maybe tomorrow. I'm going to bed.

*By the way, Langston Hughes died in New York on May
22, 1965. He had complications from prostate cancer, then
BAM! A dream interred.*

. . . .

Get it?
Good night, Swing.

All Night Long

When I wake up
after dreaming
about her,
I hear Dexter Gordon
still spinning
with static sweetness
on the record player.

I think about the way
track four, "Love for Sale,"
makes me feel,
makes me shake
and bump and thump
inside and out.
How I could listen
to it over and over again.
How if Sam wanted,
I'd give her all my love
for free.
Tie it up in a bow
and overnight it
to the front door
of her heart.

And as if I'm still
hovering between
this world
and the dream world,
I hear her laugh
coming from someplace.

I creep down the stairs,
and rub my eyes twice,
because I see that I

might not be dreaming,
that she and Walt
are talking and laughing
like it's four o'clock
in the afternoon.

What are you doing here?

Is that the way we greet our oldest and dearest friends,
Noah? Sam says, while Walt looks on with a big,
suspicious smile written all over his face.
Hey, Sam.

Hey, Noah.
What's going on here? I ask.

After you bailed on me last night, I called her and she
sounded down, so we talked for three hours, Walt says.
Want some eggs?
I thought you didn't like talking on the phone.

Well, mostly he listened. It was really special. I see why this
older girl likes our dude, Noah. He's a good listener.
Yeah, I say, shaking my head.

And then I invited her to breakfast, 'cause again, you
bailed on me, and I needed someone to help me solve a
problem.
Noah, your big party is in a week, and it's like you guys
haven't done anything.

So, you're here to help plan the party?
Sam to the rescue. It's gonna be the bash of the year, she
says. *Plus, I need something to get my mind off him.*

. . . .

But that's not even the biggest problem, Walt says.

Our dude here has gotten himself into a bit of a pickle,
Noah. Divya is taking him out on a date.
And why's that a problem?

Because I've never been on a date, so Sam's been schooling
me on what to do, how to carry myself, and all that jazz.
Oh.

251

But there's one thing I can't help him with.
Yeah, Divya's taking me to a museum, and it's one filled
with the one thing I don't know anything about. Art.

So, how can I help?
Didn't you used to paint, like, a bunch of portraits back in
third grade? he asks, winking at me.

Yeah, I remember that too, Sam says. *In fifth grade, we*
went to the children's museum on a field trip. Didn't you
make a collage during the arts and crafts lesson and—
And the teacher framed it and put it in our class. Dude, you
had some skills back then. Too bad you gave it up, he says,
winking again.

Yeah, too bad, I add.
But you loved it, and I remember you used to check out
a lot of art books from the library, so I just figured you
remembered a lot of that, and maybe you could give me a
quick lesson, he continues.

Whose book is this? Sam asks, holding up
my large, thick copy of *Art Magna:*
The World's Greatest Art, with
a suspicious smile
that I can't ignore.

Walt and I both look
at each other,
him with a smile,
me with a frown,
'cause once again
he's throwing me
a curveball
that I can't hit.

That's my mom's, I lie. Dad gave it to her for her birthday.
And I'm not even into art that much anymore, guys.

252

Noah, just give him something that'll make him sound intelligent, informed. C'mon, help Swing out.

Oh, so you're calling him that now too?
It's growing on me.

Yeah, help a brother out, Noah. Tell me about art.
Art is expression of human creativity, skill, and imagination, all at the same time, typically in a visual form such as a painting or sculpture, that uses beauty to evoke powerful emotion, I dictate from the dictionary app on my phone.

Seriously, Noah, Sam says, *we could have done that by ourselves,* running her fingers through my hair in a way that sends shudders from my ceiling to my floor.
Yeah, yo! Paint a picture for me, pun intended, he says, winking at me for the third and hopefully last time.

Art is

looking into
Mona Lisa's eyes, I say,
showing them
da Vinci's masterpiece
on page 27,
and daring her
to look back
into your soul.

Walking the midnight
sky tightrope
and dancing inside
the *Red Square*, tempting fate.

Watching *Venus de Milo*
rise out of sculpted marble,
whisper your name
as you tell her
your deepest-held
secret.

It's Monet's
Impression, Sunrise
carrying you away
on a harbor of dreams
that only God
knows about.

It's being gilded
in golden mystique
so ancient, it's new.

It's finding yourself
under the spell of
Gustav Klimt's
The Kiss,

knowing you have
your own masterpiece
inside of you,
to create the way
you want to live
if you dare
run through
the *Undulating Paths*
to find
your gifts.

It's knowing you have
this one life,
this one chance to do it
your way
before *The Physical
Impossibility of Death
in the Mind
of Someone Living*
leaves you too afraid
to find out.

Speechless Again

They both stare
at me
like deer
facing the headlights
of a car
that just came
outta nowhere.

Who are you? Walt says.
That was beautiful, Noah.

Shall I continue? I say, kinda feeling myself.
Giddyup, Picasso.

Primer Five

Look at this, I say,
showing them
page 71,
Salvador Dali's famous
Girl at a Window
oil-and-watercolor
painting.

Tell me what you see.
A girl with a big rump-shaker staring out the window,
Walt says.

You're so crass, Walt! Sam says.
Look deeper, I say, not looking
at the painting,
but at Sam,
like I've been looking at her
for seven years.
Like I've been looking
at everything
in my world:

The floor beneath us,
solid oak
like her brown eyes.

The clock on the wall,
slow, measured,
like her walk.

Look at the Dali, I say again.
Really look at it.
Tell me you do not see
a woman
looking for love

in a lavender-blue house dress.
Resting
by the window.
For a moment.
In between the laundry.
And the cleaning.
And the dinner.

Nah, yo, I don't see that at all, Walt says.
I think she's waiting, Sam adds.

Will y'all stop interrupting me, I'm on a roll.
My bad, yo.

Her name is Dream

Dream imagines
what her life would be like
if she had a dance to go to.
A man who moved
to her music.

And the people who pass by
stop and watch.
They listen
to the girl at the window.
Dream cannot see them.
She only sees the sea,
smells the hope,
dances with each wave,
takes her dreams closer
to where they belong . . .

Sounds like jazz to me, Walt says. *There's this song called*
Corcovado, *"Quiet thoughts and quiet dreams/quiet walks*
by quiet streams/and a window that looks out on—"
Dude, you're still interrupting me.
You cannot see her face, I continue,
but you know
it sings
a song of melancholy
for she will eventually
pick up her damp dishcloth
and return to the kitchen.
To her life.

Sam at the Window

That is not a dishrag,
Noah, Sam says.

It is a scarf.
This is what I see:

There is a woman
with curves that ripple

in a taut, striped indigo dress.
She is imprisoned

by trust and longing.
Everything is blue,

even the new shoes
her bare feet will not wear

again.
She is not waiting

at the window
for a man

to kill
her bliss.

She's waiting on zephyr.
She's waiting

on the cool, calm kiss
of summer

to fly her to the moon.
Which is why she has the scarf, right? I add, inspired
with opportunity.

Exactly, Noah! This is what I see, she says,
and we are both silent,

save the silent tears
falling,
until Walt does
what Walt always does.

I never thought I'd be saying this, but y'all are too deep for me. I feel like I've just made love, he says, cracking us all up. *And I'm a virgin. Dayum, art is no joke. I'm gonna see if Divya just wants to see a movie.*

Opportunity

In between
batting cages,
party planning,
listening to Walt
talk nonstop
about how Divya
smells like summer,
about how Divya
is getting a tattoo,
about how Divya
must love him, because
she wants him to meet
her parents
when they come
to visit
next year,
I spend
the next week
trying
and failing
to convince myself
to let Sam know
that I am
her secret admirer.

So, on Friday
I show up
to class
an hour before
anyone else
to tape an
anonymous love letter
under her trig desk,

only to discover
at lunch
that she and
Stephanie Wilson
switched desks.
NOOOOO!

At Lunch

The entire cafeteria
is buzzin' and poppin'
about the letter,
about Sam's secret admirer,
about the lick.

Wait, what lick?

dear love

your lips
are two sonnets
i like to link
each line
with rhyme
and repeat.

x

is what I thought
I typed.

dear love

your lips
are two sonnets
i like to lick
each line
with rhyme
and repeat.

x

is what I actually
typed.

All the Things I Want to Say

Sorry they found out,
but is that the worst thing ever?
Let them know.
Let them laugh
with envy
at what love looks like
between
two stars
inching
toward sunrise.

All the Things I Text

1:14 pm
Sorry they found out.
They're just jealous
that someone loves you
blindly and madly.

1:14 pm
That someone loves you
enough to be
anonymous.

1:15 pm
That someone loves you
more than their own
pride and ego.

1:15 pm
That someone loves you
beyond compare,
enough to take a chance
in the dark.

1:17 pm
Sorry, Sam. Text me back.
You're still coming to the party
tomorrow night, right?

Texts with Sam

11:11 pm
Nothing's real:
Art. Love. Life.

11:11 pm
What do ya mean?

11:12 pm
My hopes
have been mangled.

11:12 pm
I thought my admirer
was real.
But it's all fake.

11:12 pm
Fake?

11:14 pm
Hello?

11:16 pm
Pretend love,
like Cruz.
Everything is pretend.
The joke is on me.

11:16 pm
Maybe it
was an accident.

11:17 pm
What, my life?

11:17 pm
Stop! Come on, Sam!

11:18 pm
*I'm the joke
of the school.*

11:19 pm
I'm calling you.

11:19 pm
*No thanks.
I need to sleep this off.
Good night.*

11:20 pm
I'm sorry.
You're truly amazing.
Too good for all this.

11:23 pm
*You shouldn't be sorry.
You'd never make me
look like an idiot.*

11:23 pm
. . . .

11:24 pm
*Thanks, Noah.
I wish more guys
were like you.
Sweet dreams.*

The Party

Walt's Uncle Stanley Stanley
and two other dudes
pull up
in a van
stolen
straight out
of *Scooby-Doo.*

They jump out
in matching
red velvet jackets
with purple lapels,
unload their instruments—keyboard,
saxophone, double bass—and
find a dark corner
in the living room
to do set up
and jam, which, for now,
involves Uncle Stanley Stanley
blowing his sax, and
moving his body
like he's been electrocuted
one hundred thousand times.

10:15 pm

For the first hour
and fifteen minutes,
Walt and I
are convinced
no one is coming,
because
no one is here.
But then
they start rolling in,
with cell phones clicking
and bodies shoving me
to the side
like it's not my house.
These people,
who I see every day,
who are practically strangers,
take over.
Walt comes out with a tray of
shrimp cocktail,
fried chicken and biscuits
from Popeyes,
and some sort of punch
that some guy,
who I've never seen before,
starts immediately spiking
with a bottle
from his backpack.

10:29 pm

When Divya sashays
through the door,
Walt abandons
any sense of chill
he's acquired
from Floyd's School of Cool.
He falls into her, practically
knocking her over
with a sloppy,
nervous hug.
Oh, this is gonna be fun!

Love Is Love Is Love

This sounds really familiar, Divya says, walking into the living room.
It's a Billie Holiday composition, Walt says to her.

It sure is. WOW! You actually did it. A jazz trio. Nice touch, she says.
That's how I roll, he says. *Are you pleased?*

Beyond. I have this record in the shop. Of course, you know what's on the B-side.
Of course.

SWING, BROTHER, SWING, they both say in unison, high-fiving.
I'll leave you all to your Jazz Jeopardy moment.

I'm sorry, Noah. Here, I made a salad for the party, she says, handing me a big bowl.
Thanks, I guess.

You excited about tonight?
Yeah, should be a cool party. People are actually showing up.

No, I mean, are you going to finally tell her?
I shoot Walt a look of disgust that's becoming all too frequent. Seriously, man, you told her too. Man, you suck!

I think it's pretty sweet, Noah, Divya says. *It's the kind of thing every girl wants. Real love.*
. . . .

Love is love is love, Walt says, grinning and practically hiding behind her. *You want something to drink, Divya?*
Indeed, I do. Something heavy, she says.

. . . .

Coffee or Dew, silly, she says.

Whew! Walt says, *'cause I could never give my heart wholly and solely to a woman who imbibes. It's a waste of brain cells, and who needs it when you have imagination. I want a woman who's high on life.*

And then
they just stare
at each other
like they're enraptured,
so I walk away
to Uncle Stanley Stanley's band
jamming
to the tune of
the *Austin Powers* theme song.

Blur

People cozy
on the couch
on my patio
up the stairs.

Solo cups filled
with punch plus.

No one's
listening
to the live
elevator music,
except Walt and Divya,
which doesn't faze them
'cause it's their world
right now.

Still no Sam.

10:45 pm

A gang
of baseball players
led by Cruz
staggers in from
the backyard,
where they've been
testing the limits
of decency
in my pool.
He chugs another beer
then screams
to everyone:
LISTEN UP!

The Masquerade Is Off

I LOVE YOU, SAM. YOU'RE THE LADY OF MY
LIFE.
he yells
into Uncle Stanley Stanley's mic
like he means it,
only Sam's not even here.

The crowd is dead silent.
Except his teammates, who
hoot and holler
like he's just hit
another home run.

I'm not your lady, remember? comes a voice
from the front door.
She's here, standing
strong like Athena,
hands on her hips
with a look
on her face
that says,
I dare anyone
to mess with me
tonight,
especially you, Cruz.

She winks at me,
and we both smile
like something's about to
go down.

The Myth

I WROTE IT, Cruz hollers.
I wrote the letter
to let you know
how much
I do love you.
Let me count the ways, he continues
like he's Shakespeare reincarnated.

He licks his big,
crusty lips,
then begins to serenade her
in a blotto voice
with random clichés:

You're the apple of my eye.
You're the grass between my toes.
You're the toothpaste to my toothbrush.
You're the deodorant to my BO.

WHAT THE HECK IS THAT! Walt yells out. *Noah,*
you hear this clown with his clichés?

It gets real quiet again.
Nobody claps.
Nobody even laughs.
Everyone looks at me.
Nobody says a peep. Until . . .

Sit down, joker! You didn't write the letter, but I know
who did.
You do? Sam asks, turning around looking at Walt,
and then me.

Nerves

I look at Cruz.
I look at Sam.
I look at the blank faces.
The glaring time
on the clock.
I try not to let my lips
become bricks,
my tongue an anchor,
my mouth a desert.

Verve

There's this tune
on the *GO!* album
called *Second Balcony Jump,*
which always reminds me
of one of those old cowboy movies
where a girl
is getting harassed
at the bar
by some drunk,
then a smooth, handsome cowboy
with a thick mustache
moseys in
with his hat low
over his eyes
and utters a few
slick words:
Hey, partner, why don't you leave the lady be,
less like a question,
more like an ultimatum,
and the drunk fool will answer,
I reckon this is none of your business, stranger,
and clumsily pull out his six-shooter,
at which point
he will get shot dead
between the ears
by the handsome stranger,
who will then
ride off
into the sunset
with the lady
on his arm.

Tonight, you're the star, I say
to myself, and
this is your movie.

Writing the Story

You will reach into your pocket. And pull out a folded
piece of paper. You will open it. Because it is your destiny
to open it. Because, if this were a movie, you would be
the hunter. And if they led you to the frontier, you would
demand the ranch. And if they let you on the ranch, you
would own the farm. And if they let you own the farm,
you would take the house. And if they let you in the
house, you would take that white piece of paper, unwrap
it. And go.

And.
Go.

Reckoning

Sam, I say, softly,
the echo
frightening.

My breath quickens
like I'm swimming
from sharks,
like I'm swimming
for my life.

And then
I jump,
an ocean spilling
from my mouth.

The Wave Is Coming

Since the third grade,
when you saved my life,
I've marveled
at the pristine
masterpiece
that is you.

I am no Michelangelo.
But you are my mezza fresco.
This moment here
is my primo canvas.

I am not a superhero.
Nor a superstar.
Not Cruz or Superman.
I am just
a boy
colored by the scent
of a woman.
I am not a painter, Sam.
But I will paint you
with kindness
and passion.

I, uh—I am X.
Not because I don't want you
to know me.
But because I've always wanted you
to discover me.

PROVE IT, LOSER! Cruz yells,
speed-walking toward me
like he's up to bat
in the bottom
of the ninth

with the bases loaded.
So I reach into
my pocket
and pull out
a pitch
I've been waiting
all my life
to throw.

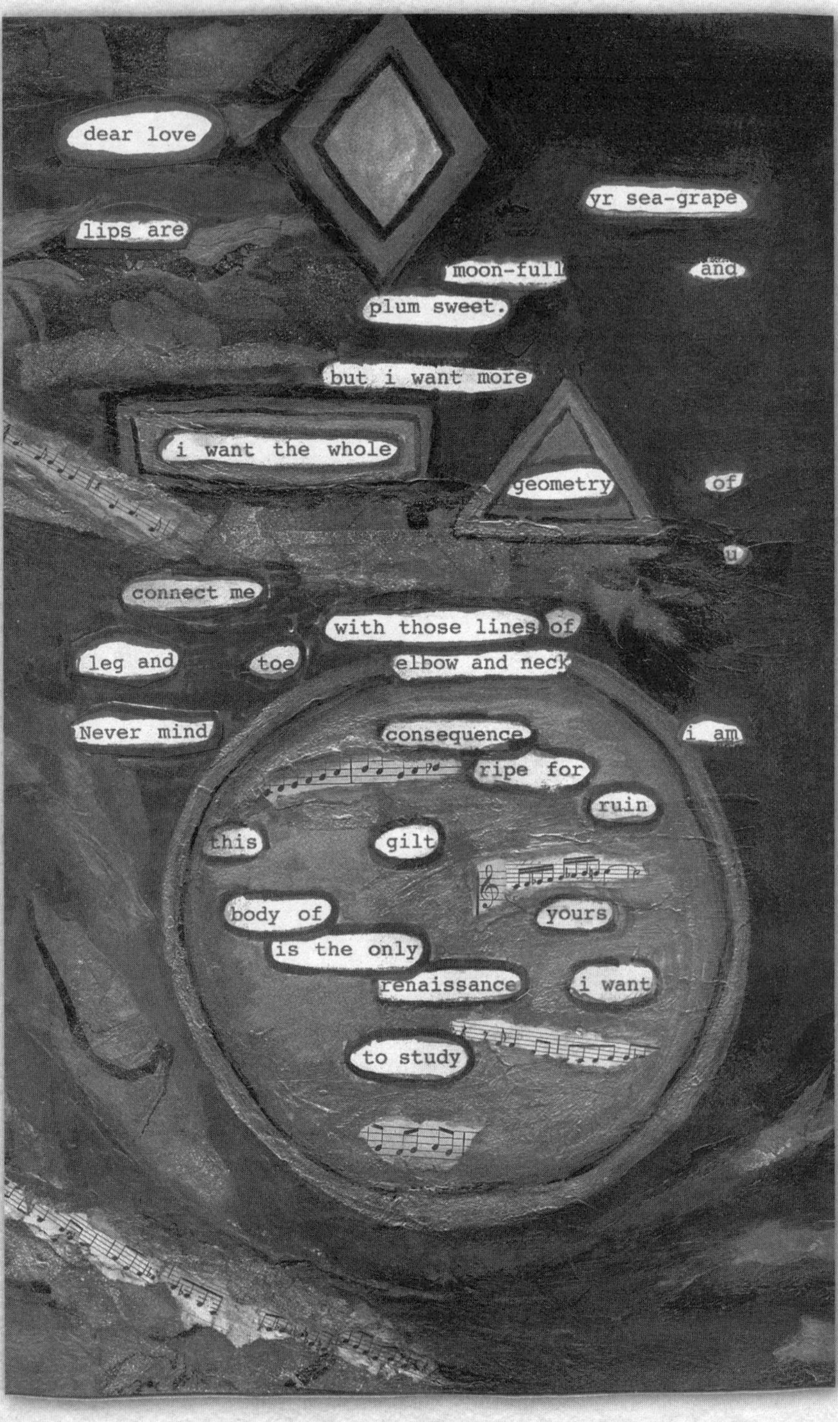
dear love
yr sea-grape
lips are
moon-full
and
plum sweet.
but i want more
i want the whole
geometry
of
u
connect me
with those lines of
leg and
toe
elbow and neck
Never mind
consequence
i am
ripe for
ruin
this
gilt
body of
yours
is the only
renaissance
i want
to study

Part 4

Love for Sale

Quiet

owns the party
again.

Then everyone roars
like I've won
an MMA match—beat
out the lone champ.

Hope Cruz doesn't pummel me.
Hope Sam doesn't leave me
ringside, wounded
and alone.

Bewildered

Eyes wide
with hesitance
and disequilibrium,
she just shakes
her head
over and over
while everyone stares.

I look at her,
Cruz looks at her,
then me,
then he frowns
and just storms
out of the house,
looking beat
for the first time
in his life.

She comes up to me,
and I don't know
if she's gonna smack me
or kiss me,
and now I can see
the sun
in her eyes
shining on me,
can feel
her arms
wrap themselves
around me,
so I do the same,
and we hug
tight
like we've never

done before,
and I feel parts
of her country
I've never traveled to,
and
she whispers,
It's you.
It's me, I say.

We Interrupt This Broadcast

Let's go outside, she says,
holding
my hand
in hers
and pulling me
into a joy
I've only
ever dreamt of.
But just before
we exit,
someone
in the family room
yells:
OH, SNAP! WHAT'S HE DOING UP THERE?!

It's a bird,

it's a plane.
No, it's a wasted
senior
on the baseball team
named Junior Wilson,
who tries
to take
a selfie video,
shirt off,
while leaping
over the railing
upstairs
onto the couch
below.

He Misses

We're crowded around
Junior Wilson
as he hollers out
like a werewolf in pain,
upstaging my night.

My back, my neck, my femur. I can't move, he hollers,
while hitting the floor with both hands and squiggling.
You're moving fine, I say. I called an ambulance.

He's gonna be all right. He's like Superman, Junior's best
friend, Will, brags. *He jumped from a roof into a pool last
year and only scraped his knees. I'll take him to urgent
care, if I need to. He probably just needs a brewsky to kill
the pain.*
If you move him, Divya says, *it will cause additional pain
and permanent injury. We should wait for the EMTs.*

The sirens

get closer
by the second.
Someone looks
out the window
and yells,

POLICE! *POLICE ARE HERE TOO!*

In less time
than it took
Junior to jump
from the balcony,
the place empties,
bodies mad-dashing,
knocking over chairs,
spilling drinks,
tearing out
the back door
and into the woods
like fugitives
of the night,
leaving me,
Walt, Divya, Sam, Junior,
and Uncle Stanley Stanley
to face
the music.

Over

The party was all Bossa
and Nova
until now.

Knock, Knock

Walt and Divya scramble
to collect party evidence.

Of course,
all the cars out front
give us away.

The knocks get louder.
I open the door.

Please, come in, I say to the EMTs. Junior's over by the
couch, I say, pointing to Junior Wilson, who's grimacing
and holding his leg.

Nightmare

Coming up
my walkway
behind
the EMTs
are two police officers,
and Cruz,
with his hands
behind his back.

BUSTED

Young man, is this your house?
Yes, sir, I answer.

I'm going to need you to fill me in on what happened.
WHY DO YOU HAVE HIM HANDCUFFED? Sam
yells, trying to run past me, but I hold her back.

That's our friend, I say.
*We got a call about a loud party going on here. Are your
parents around?*

LET HIM GO, Sam yells.
We found your friend putting a flag on a car window,
he says, pushing Cruz down on his knees. *It's a federal
offense, what he's been doing.*

*I'm assuming you're being hyperbolic, 'cause putting a flag
on a car is not a crime,* Walt says.
It wasn't me, Cruz says, visibly shaken.

*So maybe you should let him go. Like Noah said, he's a
guest.*
Was there a party here?

Sirs, we were having a get-together, Divya interjects.
Tea and jazz music. See the band right there? she adds,
pointing through the window to Uncle Stanley Stanley's
band, which is, oddly, still playing.
Why are all these cars parked out here? one of the police
officers asks us.

*One of them is my truck. I was taking the flag off of it. I
wasn't doing anything wrong, you feel me?* Cruz says.
*And why are y'all so concerned about the flags? It's just
art, right?* Sam says.

Yeah, I say, feeling the tension in the air, and not wanting

299

Sam to face it alone.
It's because he's black and in this neighborhood, isn't it?
Sam asks, less like a question, more like a fact.

Look, we don't have a problem with you. Let's not escalate this.
Your lack of imagination is the only thing that could escalate this. You probably think he's in a gang or something, right? Walt asks, making things even more tense, before Divya pulls him back inside the house.

Was he at the party? the other police officer asks me.
There wasn't really a party, sir, I lie. Just some kids hanging out, listening to jazz. But he's telling the truth—that's his truck.

How did he get hurt? the officers ask, pointing to Junior Wilson, who's being carted out on a stretcher.
. . . .

Look, we can answer questions here, or down at the station.
No one says anything,
not just because we know
there's no reason
to take us down
to the station,
but because
we're all afraid.

They Pick Cruz Up, Unlock His Cuffs, Shove Him Toward Us

I'd advise you all
to go back
in the house,
cancel any plans
you have
for your little tea party,
and if you see
or hear anything
to do with
this flag business,
you call us.
You feel ME?!

Men in Blue

Police officers
don't say *freeze*
like they do
in the movies.
They just make you
freeze in a fear
cloaked
in deep, dark dread.
And they don't
look menacing
all the time.
Some look like
they might actually
be a little gentle,
a little on the kind side.
But then
there's a gun
pinned to their hip,
that makes your heart pound
so loud,
your ears burst.
And you're not sure
what to do,
or what to say,
or how to move.
What if it's
the wrong move?
Some look so stern,
like they don't
have emotions
or a heart
that beats red.
But you wonder

if they might
smile when they're home
with their own families,
playing with their own kids.
Like the guy in front of me.
He has no expression,
but under his straight lips
and steely stare,
someone must make him smile,
someone must make him love.
He loves somebody.
He's gotta love somebody.
And I hope he remembers
somebody loves us too.

They leave us all with a warning

that almost feels
like a threat.
They leave
as if nothing
has happened.
But we all know
something has.
We stand
on the front porch
confused,
confounded,
a little terrified.
But no one shows it
more than Cruz,
who looks like
he was
beat up
and left for
the wolves.
There is an inescapable
fear in his face.
A dejected hero.
Almost like
a lost boy
in the dark.
He doesn't make eye contact
with any of us,
just crawls away
on both legs.
You should take him home, I say to Sam, not because
I want you to go with him,
but because he obviously shouldn't drive
and he obviously is broken up

right now, we all are,
and this is just the worst,
and you're the best—

No, you're the best, Noah, she says, kissing me
centimenters from
my lips,
then going after
Cruz.

Tomorrow?

The police lights
fade into the distance,
just like Sam,
as I watch her
hurry down
my driveway
to console Cruz.
They hop
into her car,
and I hear
the sad sound
of leaving
as my stomach
swallows
the longing whole.
I have no way of knowing
what will happen,
and if tonight
will mean anything
tomorrow.

I want to crawl back

into the house,
find my covers,
hide under them
until next year,
or the next.
What have I done?
Why did I let HIM win again?
I walk past Divya and Walt
curled up on the couch,
leg to leg,
arm to arm,
like two starfish.

The band finally stops, and
we all move into the kitchen,
listening
to classical music,
eating fried chicken,
leftover biscuits,
and not saying
a single word
until we hear
something crash
in the living room.

Intruder

Shhh . . . Don't talk. Don't move, Walt says, grabbing
a salad utensil,
as if he can protect us
with a wooden spork.

We huddle,
slowly ease our way
into the living room
to see, floating out there
like a living ghost
right next to
my mom's prized
(and now broken)
elephant,
Moses Jones—
Walt's big brother.

Suite for Jazz Orchestra No. 2

are the first words out
of Mo's mouth.

We stand there
dumbfounded
for a millisecond,
until Walt flies
toward his brother,
and grabs him tight.

MO!!!

I see his eyes
as he hugs Walt back.
They're vacant,
like his body
left his soul
back in Afghanistan.

Suite for Jazz Orchestra
No. 2: Scherzo

Walt brings Mo
a plate of chicken
and salad.
He slowly moves
the food around
his plate.
He keeps his headphones
plugged in his ears,
but I can tell
he hears everything,
all the small talk
and the pretend talk,
so we don't call attention
to how weird things
are getting right now.
He only responds
with a nod
here and there.

And Walt is in total denial
that there's anything wrong
with his hero,
his brother.

He looks great, doesn't he, y'all? Walt says.

Suite for Jazz Orchestra
No. 2: Lullaby

It's like he's asleep.
He looks sunken,
smells of BO,
and earth,
and night
coming fast.

Every few seconds
he jerks a little,
like his body
and mind
are on autopilot.

My big brother's home, Walt says, smiling at him. *Mo,
this is Divya, my friend, and you remember Noah, and
Uncle—*
Moses. Not Jackie. Moses. Not Jackie. Moses. Not Jackie.
Moses. Not Jackie. Moses. Not Jackie.

And Mo goes on and on like this
for minutes, until
he puts
another piece of chicken
in his mouth.
But, it's still a little awkward,
as the classical music
on Pandora
swirls
around our heads
like we're all in
a madhouse.

He's talking about Moses Fleetwood Walker, Walt
says to us. *That's who he was named after. Everybody*

thinks Jackie Robinson was the first African American
to play Major League baseball, but it was actually
Moses Fleetwood Walker. He played for the Toledo Blue
Stockings. Died of pneumonia.

BAM!
Mo screams out—
and it sounds
like a blast
from a mortar.

Suite for Jazz Orchestra
No. 2: Serenade

BAM! BAM! BAM! *I need my platoon*, he continues.
Your platoon? Walt says, looking a little scared for the first
time.

*My cocoon. My sleeping bag. My pillow. And the ground.
That's all anyone needs. When you've been sleeping in the
middle of a combat zone, that'll do.*

We all shake our heads
in agreement,
like he's making
more sense than
we've ever heard,
but he's not,
and everyone
but Walt
is royally freaked.

Yeah, man. That's all you need, I say, realizing I probably
sound ignorant, but not knowing what else to say.
I should probably roll, he says, standing and walking
toward the door.

I'll go with you, Walt says, jumping up. *Let me just grab
my stuff.*
Want me to come with you? Divya asks.

But by the time
they grab
their belongings,
Mo's gone,
disappeared, like he
was never here.

Text to Sam

12:43 am
Did you make it home?
Please let me know
you got home okay.
Walt's brother was here.

1:31 am

I reread
Corinthian's letters
to remind myself
there's no turning back
when love comes calling.
The past cannot be changed.
The future is in my hands
to be molded and shaped.
And love is a many-splendored thing.
These are all the things
I'm thinking
when
a loud knock
to my bedroom door
jolts me
back to now.

What does Walt want this time?

The Right Time

What are you doing here?
I needed to see you.

I'm glad you came back.
You sent my heart and my world spinning.

I'm sorry about everything.
I can't believe it's you. I just can't.

Well, that makes me feel good.
No, I mean, how could I have not known? Why didn't you ever tell me, Noah?

I never found the right time.
In eight years?

One day, you're in third grade, holding hands on a field trip.
I remember that.

And before you know it, the girl you love is your best friend.
You love me?

. . . .

What am I supposed to do with that, Noah?

We lie across the bed

holding hands
in silence,
staring at stars
painted on the ceiling,
and before it gets
more awkward,
I play some music.

Quiet Nights of Quiet Stars

Can we play something else?
Why? It's jazz. Just listen—it's really good.

It's a little depressing.
Give it a try. This album is great. It's Brazilian.

Can you play something American?
How about I turn it down some?

Maybe turn it off.
It's not depressing, it's yearning. It's pure pleasure. It's
magic, I say.

Yearning for what, a bullet to the head?
What do you want to hear?

Beyoncé.
. . . .

I change the music
and the subject.

How was Cruz?
I don't wanna talk about it. It's difficult. It's complex.
What went down tonight is just a lot, Noah, she says,
placing
her hand
in mine,
and suddenly
the music
doesn't matter.
Actually, nothing matters.

You okay with all this?
It's been eight years, so it's gonna take some getting used
to, Noah.

I know.

I just feel like I was thrown from a roller coaster, but I landed on a cloud. You don't think you'll land softly after a night like this. You don't think your best friend will end up being the person who has loved you all these years. And then you find yourself lying in his bed holding his hand and having heart flutters.

Heart flutters?

It's confusing, I'm going to be honest, but I'm just blown away by your art, by your words, by how you feel. It makes me feel so special, so cared about, and all I can think about is how maybe this . . . us . . . deserves a chance.

2:06 am

She texts her mom
that she's okay
and crashing
at my house,
which theoretically
is not a big deal
since she's done it
many times
over the years,
but never
like this,
so close
I can feel
her breathe.

Moon River

Her eyes sparkle
with the sacred moonlight
glowing through
the window.

She cuddles.

You're warm, she says.
My entire body is on fire,
I want to say.
It is kinda hot in here, I answer.

I open the window,
to the ghostly rustling
of trees,
like they know
the secret of how
this will all
play out.

She cuddles closer.

How was Mo?
Not good. Not good at all.

Like what?
He was spaced out, like he was here, but he was
somewhere else. And random and jerky.

You think he's on drugs?
Maybe. Also, the war. PTSD.

What does Walt say?
Nothing—it was like he didn't see it at all.

*It's his brother. Sometimes, we don't want to see the not-so-
good things happening to our loved ones.*
True.

I need to get something off my chest.
Okay. What is it?

There's something I never told you.
What is it? My heart pounds waiting for the reveal, as
if this could be something I really, really don't want to
know. Or something I do.

I tried something. Just once.
Tried what?

Weed.
That's random. Why are you telling me now?

*I don't know. We were talking about Mo, and we're here,
and I'm feeling kinda vulnerable, and I just wanted to.*
. . . .

What?
Nothing.

. . . .
What are you thinking about now?

*I like when it snows in April, like it did this year. The way
the flowers peek out from under the snow blanket.*
O-kay.

And I like taking a long nap when it rains.
I knew that.

You did not.
I've seen you nap dozens of times when it rains, and we're
supposed to be studying.

That was, like, fifth grade.
I remember.

But did you know I liked it?
I did . . . because you always look so peaceful and happy
sleeping.

322

You study me while I'm sleeping?
Ummm . . . yeah, I guess I do.

Creepy. Creepy. She uses her fingernails to crawl her
fingers through my hair. *Just creepy.* Her dancing fingers
and smile send electric bolts of thrill throughout my
body.
I know a lot about you, Samantha.

*Turns out I know very little about you, Mr. Picasso. I
should have known when you started lecturing Walt and
me on art.*
Yeah, I just knew you were gonna figure me out then.

You're a real sneaky devil, Noah Wallace.
You're a sneaky devil.

*And a brilliant artist too. They were all so beautiful, minus
the LICK, of course.*
You're beautiful, I say.

Please don't call me that.
Sorry. Why?

*What am I? How am I beautiful? Calling me beautiful
feels like a line.*
Haven't you read all my letters? Haven't you seen what
you do to me? How foolish you make me look?

She laughs,
squeezes me tight.

You're you and that's why you're beautiful. There's no one
in the world like you, Sam.
. . . .

Conversation

What's going on in there? Walt says, banging on the door.
Go away, we're making out, Sam screams.

WOOHOO! Walt screams. *I LOVE IT! ALL ABOARD*
NOAH'S ARK. ROW, ROW, ROW YOUR BOAT!
Walt, nothing's happening, I say, opening the door,
revealing Sam under the covers in my bed, and my
sleeping bag next to it.

Dude, the party was epic. Until it wasn't. The party was
outta control. Y'all good?
We're great, Sam says. *Now, can you let us get back to our*
tongue fight?

Good night, Walt, I say.
Good night? Dude, it's six am.

Huh?
If you open your curtains, you'd see that.

He shuts the door, and
we start laughing
at the wonder
and bliss
of having talked
and held hands
'til the break
of dawn.

On Monday

when we go
to get coffee,
I feel like
I own the world.

I order
for all of us
like I'm ordering
outlaws
off my ranch,
like I'm the good guy
winning the girl
and the whole
hazelnut town.
When I get
to the car,
I hand them
their coffees
and grab her hand
to make sure
I still can.
But only for a second,
'cause I can't drive
and drink
and hold
my future
at the same time.

When I get to school

it seems like there's
someone smiling
or applauding
everywhere I turn.
At my locker,
in English class,
at the library
when I return
my overdue book.

During physics, Mr. Albert,
our favorite teacher, says
there's an equation to the law
of attraction and love.
And he looks at me and smiles
as he draws it up on the board.

Even in ASL,
everybody's signing *Bravo*
and *lover boy*.

Who's da man? Walt asks himself.
Indubitably, you da man! he shouts.

I've Got You Under My Skin

I wait for Sam
after school,
and she comes out
with Walt,
and I hug her
like she's the North Star
planted firmly
in my astrology
in my astronomy
in my prayers
in my tomorrow
in my forever
in this one great, precious life.

Prelude to a Kiss

You two lovebirds should get a room, Walt says.
Wanna come back to my house? We can order pizza and
do homework, I say to Sam.

*As long as we don't have to listen to any more of that
wretched music?*
*Noah, I don't know, but you may have to nix this love
thing if she's hating on jazz*, Walt says to me, shaking his
head. *We may be too sophisticated for her.*

You calling me unsophisticated, Walt?
If the shoe fits . . .

*C'mon, Noah, let's go back to your place, and I can show
you how a sophisticated lady acts.*
I'm down for that, I say, grabbing her hand.

*Duke Ellington, May 24, 1974. Lung cancer and
pneumonia. He said, "Music is how I live, why I live, and
how I will be remembered," then BAM!*

Thanks for the history lesson. We'll see ya, Swing.
Wait, I thought we were hitting the batting cages, Noah.

I'm gonna pass on that.
You're gonna play me like that, dude?

Are you even getting better, Walt? Sam says, laughing.
I'm as good as your man is at love letters.

Then you must be exceptional, she says, kissing me on the
cheek.
Have fun, lovebirds, he says, walking away, chuckling.
Save me some dinner.

The week with Sam

is like a dream deferred
that's finally arrived.

I carry her backpack,
take her home

from school,
hold her hand

'til the streetlights
go out,

and sometimes after.
We make sugar cookies,

study for our big trig exam,
and listen to

Beyoncé so much
that I find myself

drinking lemonade,
crazy in love every day.

All I can think about is her.
All I want to do is slow dance

with her heart
in the arms

of mine.
We cuddle,

watch videos
of cats dancing,

and Junior Wilson's leap,
which has over one million views.

I take new routes
to my classes to

avoid Cruz,
but he's been missing

most of the week,
and I pray he's

dropped out.
Well, not really pray,

but hope
he's moved on.

This is my time.
This is our time.

Olive Garden

I wanted to take Sam
to Ruth's Chris steakhouse,
but *I've decided I don't do*
red meat anymore, she says,
plus it would have depleted
the cash my parents left
for me, and I already owe Walt,
so we hit
Olive Garden.

We eat bottomless salad
and breadsticks,
drink tap water,
and split a chicken parm.

I can't stop staring
at the cute way
she chews her food,
and how she
looks up at me
with those eyes
when she takes a sip
of water.

I feel like we
could do this
for a very long time,
maybe forever.

Give-and-Take

I don't care
that she doesn't do
jazz or
beef,
that she doesn't like
the way I drive
or dance, and
quite a few
other things
that I do.

All that matters
is that we
own Venus.

Are You Kidding Me?

Move over! I hear.

I look up
and see
Swing and Divya.

What are you guys doing here? You follow us?
*Ha! Thought you were strapped for cash. Didn't you beg
for me to buy you salt and vinegar chips just yesterday?*

Play nice, boys, Sam says. *Hi, Divya, nice to see you again.*
Hey, Sam. We're celebrating the big news, Divya says, as
Walt, uninvited, slides in next to me.

Celebrating what?
And next up to bat is . . .

In Full Swing

Junior Wilson,
the star outfielder,
is out
for four weeks
because he sprained
his pinky toe
trying to be Superman.

After seeing him
for the tenth time
in a row
at the batting cages,
Coach called Swing
to sub,
so now
he's playing varsity
for the rest
of the season,
and he can't stop grinning,
and he can't stop yapping
about how great
he's gonna be
way out
in left field.

After I congratulate Walt

for finally making the team,
I sit back and study
his chirpy grin
as he stuffs his face
with my breadsticks.

I'm annoyed.
Annoyed like gnats
needling my soul.

I should be excited for him,
proud of him,
celebrating him.

But, I'm annoyed.
Not salty and jealous annoyed, though.
Why couldn't I have
worked harder,
said yes more,
made the team
like Swing,
have Sam see me
as something
other than
a lovelorn artist?

I want to tell Walt
how I feel
insecure and unsettled,
share my frustration
and defeatist attitude
with my greatest counselor,
but since he's the root cause,
The Offender,
I can't tell him jack.

Plus, he'd just tell me
to embrace all the feels
and hug life.

I didn't get a call

to join the team,
but I've got her.
I've got her crimson-brown eyes
that sparkle when
I make her laugh.
I have her billion-dollar smile
she gives me
right before we kiss.
I have her soft hand
that caresses mine
when we walk.
I have her whole being
that fits
perfectly inside
my embrace
at the end of the day.
I've got my own home run.
Her.

Boundaries

What a perfect night.
It was nice, she says, putting her head on my shoulder.
I'm sleepy though.

The light turns red,
and I turn
to kiss her.

Turn right, she says.
I thought we were going to my house.

I should go home.
Why?

*Noah, let's take this slow. I know that sounds cliché . . . I
don't want this to be a Lifetime movie.*
Okay. How slow?

The Anatomy of a Kiss

It starts in a car
parked on her street
under lamplight,
the urge
to move closer.
The engine off,
windows cracked,
our shadows overlapping.

Our noses touch.
Our breath quickens.
We've kissed
at least a dozen times,
but this feels
like the first,
the only.
I'll see you next week.
You don't want to get together this weekend?

Going to see colleges with my mom.
Oh.

You're cute when you're sad. Bye, Noah, she says, leaving
me
bewitched,
bothered,
and bewildered.

Caught in a Love Haze

I'm definitely in love,
I think
as I drive
in a daze,
changing lanes
without signaling,
getting lost
on streets
I've known
for years.

I'm definitely in love,
I say
to the wind
as I slam
on brakes,
almost hitting
something—
no, someone—
running
across the street
holding a large flag.

When I get home

sitting on my front stoop,
now wearing a baseball cap
and brand-new Rams jersey,
looking beaten
and dismal
with both hands
holding up
his head,
is Baby Bonds.

I got the blues, Noah, and I got 'em bad, he says.

The Blues

You're back.
Back? What do you mean?

You haven't really been here in days.
Oh, did you miss me?

. . . .

Look, you and Sam have been doing your thing, and me and Divya have been doing our thing. We both needed our space to be in the place. But now, I got the blues.

Things with Divya good?
They were. Until, they weren't.

What happened?
I think I'm in trouble.

Why?
'Cause she kissed me.

Isn't that what you wanted?
On my neck.

Oh.
Yeah!

. . . .
. . . .

But, wait, what does that mean?
It doesn't mean she wants to engage in witty conversation and occasional verbal sparring.

She wants to—
EXACTLY! And I don't know what to do.

Well, don't ask me. My world just got rocked by a six-second kiss that felt like sixty.

I know what we need.

Please, no more Woohoo Woman!
I know exactly who we need.

Don't say what I think you're gonna say.
Let's gas up the truck and go for some dipped cones.

Seriously?

No Fries, Just More . . . Floyd

Hey, fellas, Floyd's closing. Whatcha need? Already threw the fries out.
No fries, just advice, cuz.

Floyd can do that, he says. *Heard you're playing ball.*
Yeah. And Mo's back.

Yeah, he came by. He was looking rough.
Just tired.

Nah, man, tattered, disheveled. Talked like he had heavy-ish things on his mind.
Really? Walt says.

Floyd thinks he got a little shocked over there.
. . . .

You know we were tight back in the day. We used to run things at Westside High. Floyd'll come by and holla at him. He staying with y'all?
Actually, I'm not sure where he's staying.

Cool. Anyway, what can Floyd do for you?
I got an older woman.

How old?
By two years.

That's like a dozen dog years.
Actually, it's not, I say.

Makes no never mind. So, what's the problem?
She's moving too fast for me.

Oh.
So what should I do, Floyd?

Where Floyd Tells Walt What to Do and It Makes No Sense Whatsoever

1. *Don't take her to dinner on Mondays. Everybody's in a bad mood on Mondays.*
2. *When you massage her feet, use lavender oil, not peppermint (that could be risky).*
3. *Leave her love notes on Wednesdays, but not every Wednesday, because she'll become accustomed to receiving love notes every single Wednesday, and if you ever forget, Lord, you'll be in trouble. Trust Floyd on that one.*
4. *Spring her a surprise now and again, but make sure the surprise has tickets in them. Tickets to somewhere. Or lottery tickets. Everybody needs tickets in life to feel like something special is about to happen.*
5. *Take her to the movies on Fridays, but don't buy popcorn or slushies. That's cliché and you might get bloated and gas her outta the car on the ride home.*
6. *Always keep her on her toes, switch things up, be a gentleman, and sing her songs that'll make her cry.*
7. *Eat the pizza she likes.*

But, what about how fast she's moving? Walt says.
No idea, little cousin, he says. Floyd never had to deal with that. Gotta run. Good luck, though.

Special Something

Walt is definitely unsettled,
'cause he doesn't stay up
watching movies
or listening
to music
all night.

He just plops
himself down
on the couch
and passes out,
but not before
he says,

Oh, I forgot to give you something.
What?

Sam told me to hide it in your room or somewhere, but I'm
too exhausted. Here, he says, handing me an envelope.
Good night. Gotta be ready for the big game Tuesday.
We're tied for first place.
Thanks, I say, taking the envelope.

Did you hear what I said, yo? We're. In. First. Place.
Yay.

Phone Conversation

Whatchu doing?
Thinking of you.

Awww, that's sweet.
. . . .

How'd you like my masterpiece?
I give you a B+

WHAT! I put a lot of work into that!
Just kidding.

It's like a recipe for love.
Yeah, I got that.

You're mean.
Seriously, thank you for it. I love it. You don't know how
much I love it.

*Well, you made me feel special when I wasn't feeling so
great, and I wanted to thank you for showing me how
much you care.*
Care . . . you're more than someone I care about.
Sam . . . I love you. I love you so much.

She's silent.
Just long enough
for me
to feel awkward.

Hey, Walt's big game is next week. You coming with me?
Of course, wouldn't miss it for anything.

What about this weekend? What should we do?
*Do you even listen to me? Remember, my mom's taking me
to some colleges.*

Oh, yeah.

Talk tomorrow, Noah. Bye.

Don't go yet.

. . . .

Click.

The Big Game

As we wait
on the bleachers
for the game
to start, it's
an unbelievable feeling
to have
my girl
by my side when
I'm getting ready
to cheer my
best friend.

Feels like
rebirth.
Smells like
her wild orchid perfume
and tastes like
salted pretzels,
popcorn, soda,
Skittles.

I can't believe this is Walt's first high school game. He's
been dreaming of this day since I met him, I say, pouring
Skittles into my mouth.
*It's incredible. A testament of his perseverance. It's a good
quality to have. We all could use a little more of what
Walt's got.*

Yeah. I guess you're right, I say, inching closer and
throwing my arm around her.
*I really care about you, Noah. Your friendship has meant
the world to me all these years.*

She takes a handful
of popcorn,

shoves it
into her mouth,
and chomps
like she didn't just say that.

Friendship?
I thought
we moved past
the friendzone
when we kissed
for the eightieth time
this morning,
is what I'm thinking.
But I don't say a word.
Instead, I ride out
the awkwardness,
hold her tight.

Realization

In our silence,
with the sound of
the baseball team gathering,
it occurs to me she might sense
that there's something about all of this
that's a fraud,
and that might be
what's holding her back
from loving me too.

Caught in the Truth

Sam, there's something I've got to tell you.
Okay.

Walt gave you the first one.
The first what?

The first love letter.
WALT WROTE THEM?

NO! He just gave it to you. It was his idea.
Oh.

I'm sorry. I was just a little scared.
But, you wrote it, so—

So, those first few letters I gave you, I didn't exactly write
them all by myself—I found letters from the sixties by a
guy named Corinthian, picked out the words that spoke
to me, then I created the art.
*Wait. What? You didn't write any of them? And who in the
world is Corinthian? How did you get his letters?*

I wrote some of them, just not the first couple. I mean, I
borrowed—
I'm confused, Noah. Did you write them or not?

I found these love letters in the Keepall I gave my mom
for her birthday. They were hidden underneath a tear at
the bottom of the purse. So, mine were inspired by this
dude named Corinthian, who wrote love letters to his
girlfriend back in the 1960s.
. . . .

But all the latest ones, the ones I read you at the party,
the ones I read to you in front of everyone to express how
I feel . . . those were completely mine, Sam.
. . . .

I'm sorry, Sam.
I'm glad you told me.

You mad?
Just confused. If those weren't your words, then—

But it was my art. My heart. My. Every. Word. Every
color. Every ounce of me was on those pages.

. . . .

You are mad.
I'm okay.

She says
she's okay,
so why do I feel
like a child
who's just been caught
cheating
or stealing?

Love is a many-splendored thing,
and there's no going back
on the truth,
are the things
I'm thinking
when Cruz comes up
to bat.

The Last Inning

Her eyes move
to the batter's box,
where he stands
like some kind of baseball god.
I take her right hand into mine.
It feels cold.
I rub my thumb
over her knuckles.

I look at her face
as she watches his
every move.
Her faint smile
dances
across her lips
at him, just
in time
for him to
look our way
and wipe his brow,
the way he's done
in every game
before, like
it's a secret signal
between them.

She waves
with the hand
I held
inside mine
mere seconds ago.
The one
that I've loved
for seven summers.

Why does it feel
like I'm in the last inning
of a game
that hasn't even started?

Debut

The game is slow.
The company, aloof.
It seems to take five
long, dreadful nights
before Walt actually
gets to bat.

He struts out wired,
lit like a firecracker
that's about to go off.
Bopping his head
to the jazz
that's undoubtedly playing
inside it.
He looks authentically
confident.
Sam and I both jump up,
applaud like
it's his curtain call
and this is *Hamilton*.

He taps the bat
on the ground.
His swing looks good.
Then the ball comes
fast and furious
like a cannonball.
Not once.
Not twice.
But three times.
And he misses
each.
On his way back
to the dugout,

he looks up at me, and
I raise my fist
as if to say,
you got this,
but I'm not sure
he does.

The Ride from Antarctica

We don't talk
or whisper
or even sigh.

Shivers come over me.
It's the kind of silence that
makes you cold.

It's just a painful void,
louder
than torture itself.

My mind races
with uncertainty.
Are we okay?

Is she sick?
Or just sick of me?
What do I say?

I pull up to her house,
and put the car
in park.

More silence.
I turn to face her,
to tell her

how I am
the sun to her moon,
when suddenly

she leans
and plants a kiss
on my cheek.

Forlorn

Mom and Dad
are coming home
early next week.

Walt is hanging out
with Divya, daily,
and I'm sitting here
feeling kinda lonely
and unsure, 'cause Sam
is on an overnight field trip.
And so is Cruz.

I start thinking
about my future,
and how maybe
I've got nothing
going on.

What if I end up
like Floyd,
dipping ice cream cones,
recording podcasts,
and pretending
to have
a life?

Texts with Granny

5:07 pm
Hey, Granny.
I need to talk,
can we hang?

5:07 pm
You can come over.
Or I can come over.
Pimento cheese sandwiches?

5:10 pm
We can binge watch
The Crown.

6:18 pm
SORRY, SUGAR.
I BEEN PLAYING POKER
WITH SOME SHYSTY FELLAS.
YOU NEED SOMETHING?

6:19 pm
I just missed you, Granny.
Figured we could get
together before Mom
and Dad get back home next week.

6:21 pm
AWFUL!

6:21 pm
Huh?

6:23 pm
i wrote aww! but it changed
my aww. noah, how do i
fidget . . . see it did it again. FIX!

6:24 pm
THIS ONE FELLA FLIRTS
WHENEVER HE'S BUFFING.
I'M ABOUT TO CALL HIS . . . MEAT
BLUFFING. MEANT. NOAH HELLLPPP!

6:25 pm
NOAH WALLACE HAS LEFT THE CONVERSATION.

WOOHOO WOMAN
Podcast #6: Outro

MARJ: *You crack me up, Jackie! But seriously, before we get out of here, I want to run this by you. I read this quote in a book: "To receive love, you have to give it, and in order to give it, you have to have it." Okay, maybe I'm a little slow, but how can you give something you don't have? Or how can you have something you don't have, or . . . see, I'm confused, Jackie!*

JACKIE: *Hmmm. It sounds like a riddle for life. I think I get it though. Receive, give . . . when I really think about it, it means you have to love yourself first. If you don't love yourself, how can you possibly love others? You feel me?*

MARJ: *I DO. I DO. Without self-love, you have nothing to offer others. Friends. Family. Lovers. A Woohoo Woman knows this. It is her mantra.*

JACKIE: *Speaking of self-love, ladies. Get out there today and do something nurturing for yourself, and then you can go out into the world and love others.*

MARJ: *Here's to a nap. Next week, we're taking a surprise road trip and dipping our toes into new waters.*

JACKIE: *Ooooh, are we podcasting from the beach? Jamaica? Cancun?*

MARJ: *Floyd, you listening? We want the beach.*

JACKIE: *Loyal listeners, tune in next week to* The Woohoo Woman Podcast *to find out where in the world Jackie and Marj have landed.*

Text from Sam

10:10 pm
Miss you, Noah. I'm
back tomorrow, but then gone
for weekend with Mom.
Let's get together Sunday night.
Smooches.

Dear Sam

without u
i am lost
as in: isolated
unfin-
ished
broken
off
shipwrecked
on the shore
of solitude
ankle
deep
   in
        possibility
i have read the dictionary
twice
i. have. read. the. dictionary.
twice.
and still there r no words
to fill
my blank spaces
to punctuate
the way i feel
with yr smile
two-steps
across the stucco walls
of my memory

perhaps
i will open
a thesaurus now
and find
a little piece of hope
or something similar.

in other words
i miss you.

ps. All I've done since you left is write and draw. You like the piece? I call it *Hand to Hand*. Walt says I should submit it to this contest at a local gallery. If you're okay with it, I might.

Do not forget me.

Love, Noah.

On days like this
when the stinging wind
of solitude
blows by,
I miss
the warmness
of my hand
inside yours,
each finger
a lifeline
of calm.

Text to Walt

Swing, let's hang out.
Go to the mall.
Hit the batting cage.
Have a lazy Saturday.
I need to get out
of my head
and this house.

Text from Walt

11:45 am
Yo, I can't.
Divya and I
are out looking
for some hip glasses
and a tux,
'cause yeah,
I'm going
to the prom.
Guess who just found cool?

Something Is Coming

You know how things
are going great
and life feels easy
and joyful,
and then you get
that sensation
that something's at your back,
but nobody's there—an
empty feeling
hangs in the air
and everything looks gray,
even the sun?
When it feels like
something is about to
pull you under
and you're afraid
to move
or breathe?
That's where I stand.
Right now.
And, it's not good.
It's not good at all.

Part 5

Where Are You?

Conversation with Walt

Yo, my dad's home.
For the wedding?

*Heck no. Mo showed up at the house a few days back and
he slept over, and Mom said he had nightmares all night,
and when she went in to check on him, he was in fatigues
holding a bat and just staring at her. Through her.*
Dang, yo!

*Then he just left. She got scared and called my dad to
come find him.*
Where is he?

I think Mo and Dad are at a hotel.
Oh.

*He'll be fine. He just needs rest. Mo will be back better
than ever!*
. . . .

Hey, you like the tux? he asks, unzipping the garment bag
he's carrying.
It's fire.

*Black pants, white jacket, red cummerbund. I'll be the
dopest, flyest in the house.*
. . . .

You know you can come with us.
Nah, I'm good. Plus, my parents are home on Tuesday.

*Okay then, but can you stop looking so sad? Dang, you're
killing my life high.*
I miss her.

Dude, go see her then.
She's out of town, until tonight.

*Well, she must have a twin then, 'cause Divya and I saw
her earlier today after I left the weight room.*
Where?

At the mall.
. . . .

Texts to Sam

Sunday, 2:00 pm
Sam, you home?
Walt says you're back
in town.
How was your trip?
Miss you.
Call me.

Sunday, 2:45 pm
Where are you now?
Want me to come by?

Sunday, 3:15 pm
Hello?
Wanna come over here?

On the drive

to her house,
there's bumper-to-bumper
traffic
on Main Street.
When I get out
to see the problem,
I see an empty grocery cart
on its side—trash, bags,
and countless flags
scattered—in
the middle
of the intersection,
and a bunch
of police officers.

When the traffic clears

I drive
to Sam's house
to find her mom's car
in the driveway,
and her little Brussels griffon
sitting
by the screen door,
on guard.

I'm relieved
she's home,
then I'm not,
when I realize
she's been home
and she hasn't
acknowledged my texts,
called me,
or told me
she's actually back.

And when I ring
the doorbell,
and Cruz opens
the door,
I'm pissed.
ROYALLY.

How Long Has This Been Going On?

What are you doing here, Cruz?!
The question is, what are you doing here, Noah? The
answer is, trying to steal my girl with your sappy little love
notes.

Give me those, Sam says, coming up behind him,
snatching the letters.
You can't be me, kid. You'll never be me, so why don't you
go on home.

Sam? What's going on? I ask.
I'LL TELL YOU WHAT'S GOING ON, NOAH, Cruz
yells at the top of his lungs, his hot breath an inch from
my face.

But I don't hear
what he's yelling,
as I plot
my next move:
Shove
my fist
in his face
and risk
being left the loser,
bloodied.
Or leave.
Walk away,
broken.

Escape

I run
back to my truck,
almost stumbling.
Get in,
try to back out
of her driveway,
but she's standing behind
blocking me,
with her arms folded
and her legs parted wide,
in a stance
that lets me know
she's not moving.

Get out of the truck, Noah!
Will not.

C'mon, I have your other shoe.
Not as long as he's here.

Cruz, go. I'll call you.
Okay, babe, but don't be long, I hear him say.

I sit behind
the steering wheel
and close my eyes
for a moment
that feels
as raw
as an open wound,
wishing
I could be
someplace else,
someone else,
not having to deal

with the drama
that's coming
or the pain
that's here.

Another Reckoning

I finally get out
of the truck
after I hear Cruz
speed off.

I lean against
Granny,
who's been more faithful
to me
than her.

Sam reaches out
for my arm,
like she's trying
to pull me in
for a hug,
but I resist.
I pull back and stand
as still
and as cold
as a glacier.

Let's go inside.
I'm fine out here.

I want to talk someplace private, quiet.
Maybe I don't want to talk. Period.

End

I open
my truck door,
she shuts it.
I open it again,
push my way
inside.

If you leave— she says.
WHAT, YOU'RE GONNA BREAK UP WITH ME?
TOO LATE! YOU ALREADY DID THAT, I shout.

I'm not
going to stand
for betrayal.
I'm not going
to listen
to her lies,
to let her
talk about
how she feels
anymore.

What about how I feel?
I've had enough.
Got enough fumes
to fuel this truck
for the rest
of its sorry life.
So, I speed off,
leaving her
standing there,
'cause there's nothing else
to hear,
absolutely nothing else

to say, but
goodbye, Sam.
I'm done.

Early

The door
wide open
and suitcases
on the front porch
tell me
they're back
from Spain,
and I'm gonna
have to act
like I'm happy,
which I'm just not
right now.
That instead
of wallowing
in despair,
which is what
I'd really like
to do,
I've got to act
like I'm ecstatic
they came home
two days early.

Hey, welcome back, I say, hugging Mom.
Hey, honey, Mom says, kissing me on the forehead.

We need to talk, Dad says.
Am I getting another car? I say sarcastically, hugging
him.

Nope, Mom counters, *but where is my vintage brass Asian
elephant?*
Dad follows with, *And where is your grandmother?*

Consequence

I don't snitch on Granny, but I'm so troubled, I don't
deny that Mom's coveted elephant from Thailand
is missing its tusks, and that I hid the elephant away
because Moses knocked it over . . . that I had a party . . .
that Junior Wilson jumped from our balcony and fell
hard, but that he and his pinky toe will survive . . . I
tell them how the party was all to impress Sam . . .
That I confessed my love to her, for her . . . I tell them
how she loved me back . . . and now she doesn't . . . I
tell them how prom is never going to be in the cards
for me . . . How Walt is going . . . How Walt made the
baseball team . . . How life sucks . . . and they end up
not punishing me . . . because I guess my parents have
decided my life is punishment enough.

Kind of Blue

I heard the news today
that my life is over.
Destroyed
in one afternoon.
I watch the record
spin round and round
to the sound
of my love drowning.
You don't matter
to her anymore.
Freddie Freeloader
is who she really wants,
and you were just
a rebound.
The sax, trumpet,
piano, and drums
taunt me,
haunt me,
scream at me.
Keep listening,
they holler.
We know you.
These songs were
composed from
my pain.
Blue in Green—
everything will
turn to frozen blue.
The bass says,
You're a fool,
as it keeps the rhythm
of my tears.
Flamenco Sketches

of her in my mind.
I heard the news today.
She's over.
We're over,
and it's *All Blues*.
All Blues
for the rest
of my sorry days.

Part 6

Three O'clock in The Morning

Text from Walt

1:32 pm
You coming to the game?
I'm feeling lucky, like
it's gonna be epic.

Two Strikes

Walt swings
at two fastballs
like he's swatting
flies at a picnic,
wondering
if he connected,
the crashing pop
of ball
in leather
telling us all
he didn't.

Walt at Bat

The outlook is dismal for Walt Disney Jones today:
two strikes and three balls, I doubt he makes the play.
Divya clings to hope: *If only he could get a whack at that—*
It's do or die for my Swing at bat.

All eyes on Walt as he digs his hands in dirt;
two tongues holler when he wipes them on his shirt;
and now the pitcher launches a nightmare
and Baby "Swing" Bonds misses everything but air.

"Strike one!" the umpire roars.
With a sneer, Walt assures he's got something in store.
The second Mercury moon comes spinning through;
he swings . . . and the umpire yells, "Strike two!"

The smile is gone from Walt's lip;
upon his cocky shoulder, a chip.
And now the pitcher winds for the throw;
and now the air is crushed by my best friend's blow.

Oh, somewhere jazz is playing, and love is in full flight.
And in this tiny town, a flag is flying bright.
And somewhere men are fighting, living in combat.
But there is joy today at Westside—because Walt's at bat.

Unfortunately

When the next pitch
comes,
Walt smacks it

into the outfield!
Me and Divya—with
her new, matching

HUG LIFE tattoo—
jump up as if
it's a miracle.

She starts
snapping pics
like a proud parent.

Swing jumps
for joy,
kicking dirt,

running
for first base,
and that's when

I realize,
and I'm sure he does too,
that he should have been

practicing
running
as much as batting,

because as fast
as he swung
and hit that ball,

he gets thrown out.

Independence Day

*Yo, I got a hit. Did you see it? I killed it. I go up to bat. I
miss the first pitch, the second, then BAM.*
I know, Swing. I was there. Remember?

I don't even care that I didn't get on base. I hit.
Indeed, you did.

It's happening, Noah. Right now.
What?

I've hit my stride.
Oh, really? How's that?

I've discovered the secret to success.
Yeah, what's that?

*Life is not easy for any of us. But what of that? We must
have perseverance and be arrogant in our self-love. We
must believe that we are gifted for something and that this
thing must be attained.*
That's actually deep, Swing.

It was deep when Marie Curie said it too, Divya says,
kissing him on the cheek.
*First woman to win a Nobel Prize, first person to win
twice,* he says, turning his cheek and catching her on the
lips.

For inventing radiation, right?
*For developing the theory of radioactivity that allowed
us to actually understand how radiation works.
Unfortunately, she got exposed to too much radiation, and
BAM. July 4, 1934.*

At least she died doing what she loved, Divya says, and
they both laugh and link arms, like they were meant to
be, like nothing else matters, like they own the world.

Hey, was Sam here?

Didn't see her, Divya says. *Did you, Noah?*
No, I say nonchalantly, trying to act like I didn't notice, when I most definitely did.

Texts with Walt

5:14 pm
*Yo, since you're not going
to prom, and I am,
can I borrow your car?*

5:14 pm
Uh, no.

5:18 pm
*I'll knock that interest off
your IOU.*

Future Plans

On the way
to get Granny
detailed,
'cause he says
my car is appallingly
filthy,
he casually mentions
that he might graduate early,
this summer,
then travel
around the world
before heading to
his dream school,
Grinnell College—
Because they had a black graduate
in eighteen freakin' seventy-nine.
That's where I need to be. Right
in the middle of an institution
that reeks of social justice
and progress.
You feel me, Noah?
Yeah, I feel you.

Also, because Herbie Hancock went there.
I'm assuming he's still alive.

At the Stoplight

Hey, isn't that—
It is. Don't look.

Just drive then.
I can't—the light's red, dude.

She's rolling down her window. She's—
Hey, guys!

Ignore her. Act like we don't hear her.
My window's down, Noah.

GUYS! Pull over.
Oh, hey, Sam, Walt says.

Hey, yourself. Pull over, I need to talk to Noah.
Sure thing.

Why'd you say okay?
What was I supposed to say, Noah? She was literally right next to us.

Conversation with Sam

Are we okay?
It is what it is.

What does that mean?
It means sure, we're friends, okay?

Then why've you been ignoring me?
Not ignoring, just busy.

All day and night.
Homework. Parents are back. Everything's not about you,
you know.

You're still mad.
. . . .

Talk to me.
What do you want me to say?

*I want you to say we're still friends. That you're mad, but
you'll get over it. That we really don't have anything in
common. We don't like the same music, the same food. It
was nice and fun and a little mysterious, but you gotta
admit, we really didn't gel.*
. . . .

Say something, Noah.
So you're gonna be with him now?

*I don't know. No, maybe. It's complicated. But I know what
I'm not gonna be.*
What's that?

*One of those girls who makes a dumb decision 'cause she
thinks a boy won't like her anymore and the rest of her life
is screwed up.*
. . . .

400

*I'm not gonna be the girl that's known a boy forever and
ruins that relationship because she thought that they were
lovers who were friends, instead of best friends who loved
each other. I don't wanna lose you, Noah.*
Then why'd you do that to me—why'd you lie?

*I didn't know what to do. It was stupid. I'm sorry I hurt
you, Noah. I'm still trying to figure out what love is.*
You should listen to jazz.

. . . .

So, you think we're gonna be better being friendly
instead of romantic?

We were for eight years.
What about our kisses?

What about them?
Were they okay?

They were more than okay. I liked kissing you.
Well, you could use a little work keeping your teeth to
yourself, I say, with a smirk.

Oh, you got jokes, do you? she says, plucking me.
. . . .

I'm sorry, Noah.
You didn't have to throw it in my face, Sam.

*I didn't mean to. Cruz just showed up. We talked a few
times and he wanted to get back with me, but I wasn't
ready. He just came over with some flowers, like that was
gonna work.*
Did it?

I don't know. I mean no.
Well, I just want you to be happy, for real.

That's why I love you.

401

A lot of good that does me now.

. . . .

I'm just kidding. We're good.

You sure?
Yep, just don't tell Walt that you broke up with me. Tell him it was mutual. I gotta protect my street cred.

Your street cred? That's funny.
We gotta finish cleaning the truck. Walt's taking it to prom. You going?

Yeah.
With Cruz.

Not with him, but yeah.
That sounds real suspect.

. . . .

Well, goodbye, Sam.

Don't say it like that—it sounds so final.
Have fun tonight.

It's definitely over

I tell Walt, but we're cool.
You sure, yo?

Wasn't meant to be, but it hurts a little. A lot more than a
little, actually.
Sorry, dude. I guess she wasn't your soulmate after all.

At least you found yours.
True, and I need to get home so I can practice.

Practice?
Cooking.

Huh?
I'm cooking her dinner for prom.

No way.
*Tandoori chicken, this chickpea dish I saw on Top Chef,
and samosas.*

You know how to make all that stuff?
*I want to be a full human. I love new ideas. And new
people. I want her to know I respect and honor her culture.
Real diversity begins at the dinner table. Our humanity,
Noah, will rise with our breaking of daily bread. You
must—*

Okay, okay, I get it.
It's about to go down, Noah.

Just don't mush up all your food in front of her, yo.
My uncle's band is gonna serenade her.

Uncle Stanley Stanley is back in effect.
*I got a playlist and everything. Watch out, world, Swing is
coming through like gangbusters.*

All the Things You Are, Divya: A Playlist by Swing

Come Rain or Come Shine
You Go to My Head
All of You
You and the Night and the Music

The Way You Look Tonight
I Don't Stand a Ghost of a Chance
There is No Greater Love
It Had to Be You
You're My Thrill

Someday Sweetheart
Over the Rainbow
East of the Sun and West of the Moon
Let's Fall in Love
Just You, Just Me
Bumpin' on Sunset
A Love Supreme

Slowly Coming Alive

For the next
few days
I catch up
with Mom,
do extra credit
for physics class,
practice writing essays
for the SATs,
even make it to
the batting cage,
just to hit
some frustration
into the air.

But the best
part of my week
is taking
the fifty dollars
Mom gave me
to the thrift store,
to buy a couple
Coltrane albums,
ephemera of all kinds,
and an art kit
that's never
been opened.

What Being Alone Looks Like

There are hundreds
if not thousands
of photos
and videos
being plastered
online.

Everybody's got a date.
There's Walt and Divya
shutting down
the dance floor.
Cruz and Sam
laughing
like everything's
back to normal.
Everyone's either
smiling or smirking,
twirling or twerking,
posing or posturing,
kissing or wanting.
And I'm here
playing solitaire.

Best Thing I Never Had

I stop
torturing myself,
get offline,
and fall asleep
listening
to Beyoncé
'cause even though
it is what it is,
I still miss
what isn't.

Why is my alarm

going off
at three o'clock
in the morning?

Because it's not—
it's my phone
buzzing.

Who's calling me
this late?

Stranded

Hello?
Yo, wake up.

Who is this?
It's me, Swing.

Who?
It's me, Walt.

Walt, what are you doing?
Your truck stopped.

What do you mean, it stopped?
Dude, it won't move. It won't start.

Did you put gas in it?
Of course I put gas in it. Can you come get me? It's cold and dark out here.

Where are you?
Alaska, maybe, I don't know. I dropped Divya off. She lives way out.

. . . .
You there, Noah?

Yeah, I'm here.
I'll drop you the pin on Google Maps.

Walt, you have my truck. How am I supposed to get there?
Take your parents' car. They won't mind, it's an emergency. Help a brother out.

. . . .
You coming?

I leave

my parents
a note,
take the keys
to Dad's car,
and drive out
to the middle
of nowhere.

Let's Face the Music and Dance

You're listening to Diana Krall.
Huh?

The music. It's a great song.
I just turned it on. I wasn't really paying attention.

There may be trouble ahead/But while there's music and moonlight/And love and romance/Let's face the music and dance, he sings. She's no Sarah Vaughn, but what a voice, yo.
Great, now let's call a tow truck or something.

What took you so long?
Takes a minute to get to Alaska.

Dude, it's not safe way out here.
Looks pretty safe to me. This is a nice neighborhood.

Yeah, pretty safe for YOU, but I'm a black kid walking up and down the street with a baseball glove. At three am. In the middle of nowhere. You do that math, Noah. A storm is coming.
It's not raining.

But it's coming. Look at the halo around the moon.
You and your freakin' superstitions.

Oh, the storm is coming, Noah. Let's get out of here. We can get it towed in the morning.
My parents are gonna freak.

I need some coffee, bad.
Why do you have your glove with you, by the way?

Gotta break it in. Doctors have stethoscopes, I got a glove.
. . . .

Noah?
Yeah?

411

I think I died tonight.
Huh?

Divya kissed me, really kissed me, and it was an out-of-body experience. It was heaven, Noah, and she was an angel.
I see.

We danced all night, drenched in sweat and passion, then went outside to cool off. I was in the middle of confessing my endless love for her when she leaned in and kissed me, and everything was LIT UP—the stars, my eyes. I literally felt my soul leave my body and dance in the sky.
That's pretty intense. What happened next?

. . . .

Walt, what happened next?

Noah, pull over.
Huh?

NOAH, PULL OVER NOW!
WHAT?

The Flag Bearer

Next to a park
on a baseball field,
swinging a bat
at an imaginary ball,
and surrounded by
flags staked
in the ground
like a shield,
is a guy
in army fatigues
screaming
"The Star-Spangled Banner."

Wandering
in this desert
is Walt's brother,
Moses.

MO!

Walt screams,
jumping out
of the car
before it even comes
to a complete stop.

MO! WHAT ARE YOU DOING?! Walt yells,
running the field,
picking up the flags
along the way.

I follow him.

IT'S ME, he screams
to Mo, who doesn't see us,
just the sky
he's still swinging at,
which is now
crying a river,
just as Walt predicted.

MO, IT'S ME. IT'S ME, WALT!

Haunting

We stand there
under hammering rain
face to face
with a ghost,
who doesn't speak,
just stares
through us.

Hey, Mo, I say, you okay?
What are you doing out here? Walt says, taking the bat
from Mo.

He watches us
like we're trespassing
on his life.
Walt goes to hug him,
but Mo starts
turning in circles,
yelling, *mine*, mine, MINE,
hopping
like there are bombs
beneath us.

I go back to the car,
to get the umbrella
I hope is in the trunk.

I see Walt
grabbing Mo,
embracing him.
Then, I hear sirens.
And, the explosion
comes fast
and hard
like a pitch
you never saw coming.

Out of nowhere

six cops out
of nowhere six
cops erupt out
of nowhere six cops
erupt with
out of
nowhere six cops erupt
with commands out
of nowhere
six cops erupt
with commands and out
of nowhere six
cops erupt with
commands and
guns out
of nowhere.

BOOM!

I
    hear
blue
    lights
Mo
    screams
Panics
    Runs
Walt
    follows
Too
    late
Mo
    ghost
STOP
    NOW
COP
    YELLS
HANDS
    UP
Walt
    freezes
I
    stare
at
    Walt
then
    cop
looks
    scared
DON'T
    MOVE
they

say
Rain
    fast
Hits
    ground
Six
    Cops
White
    noise
Point
    guns
at
    Walt
ON
    GROUND
RIGHT
    NOW
He
    drops
bat
    first
One
    shoots
two
    shoot
three
    shots
slice
    through
rain
    drops
Walt
    drops
blood
    drops

I
    run
I
    run
to
    Walt.

War Zone

Before I can get
to him
before I can save him
before I can let them know
that they've made a mistake
that he's Walt Disney Jones,
The King of Swing,
the Sultan of Smooth,
the Count of Cool,
a cop
tackles me
like I'm a running back
and he's a linebacker,
only this isn't a game,
and there is no referee
to keep my face
out of the dirt
and my ears from ringing
from the bomb
that just dropped
on my life.

Witness

I sit
in the police station
staring at a checkered wall,
each block
a different memory.

The policemen,
slow, yet anxious
in their approach.

The wind
bouncing
the rain
from tree to dirt.

The bat falling
from Walt's hands,
suspended
for too long.

The sound
of gunshot
piercing air
and flesh.

The way Walt wobbled,
the way his legs gave,
the way he dropped
like falling leaves
from a soaring tree.

One of them who fired.
The blond crewcut one,
whose cap fell
to the ground, after.
The one who rushed Walt,

then cuffed him.
After.

I sit
in the police station
waiting for my parents,
trying not to remember
before.

Interrogation

I sit
with my dad
until it's almost daylight,
answering questions
about a crime
committed
by the people
asking the questions.

What were you doing out there?
He was my friend.

What was he doing in the park?
Why'd you shoot him?

Why'd he have the weapon?
He had a bat. A BAT!

That's a weapon.
NOT ON A BASEBALL FIELD.

. . . .

Don't say anything else, my dad says, holding back
the tears.
I think we're good here, says the police officer.

Says Me

We are not
good here, no
good. We are not
good. You are not
good here. You are not
God. Here. You are
not God. You
are no God. You
    are no good. Here.
    You are not good
    here. We are not.
Good.

After

Dad wants to
take me home
to shower
to eat
to not remember
the sorrow,
to begin
to climb
the volcano
of mourning, but
there is only one place
I want to go.
Need to be.

Critical Care

I walk in,
see tubes.
Lots of them.
A muted television.
Cards from classmates.
His mother and father
and future stepfather
in and out
of the room.
A record player
that Divya brought in
sitting in the corner
playing *Birth of the Cool*
over and over.

And, Swing.
Barely smiling.
Barely here.
My tears collecting
on my shirt,
falling on Swing's
hospital bed.

Autumn Leaves

You never paid me back, yo, are the first words out of his
mouth.
I'm going to. I promise. I'm going to pay you back double
someday.

It was Moses . . . The flags.
I know. I was there, I was with you, I say.

Sam was here. Crying. Like you.
I'm sorry, Walt. I'm so—

Everything is copacetic, he says, like he really believes it.

I grab his hand.
There is blood between us,
inside our grip.

Are you my best friend?
Ride or die.

Ride AND die, apparently, he says, trying to laugh, but
coughing. *You still owe me, for the loan.*

A nurse comes in
to keep
what's left
of the river
in his veins
from pouring out.

My tributaries are in a mad rush, yo, he says, each word
sounding fainter. *They can't stop the bleeding inside.*
. . . .

Hey, Noah?
Yeah?

What's today?

427

Monday.

Monday? That sucks.
What? What's wrong.

I was hoping it was Friday. All the good ones go on Friday.
Chet Baker, Duke Ellington.

. . . .

It's okay, Noah.
No, it's not. It's not okay. Those cops are gonna pay. All
of them are gonna pay. I prom—

Are you my best friend, Noah?
Yeah.

Then do me a favor.
A favor. Yeah, what? Anything!

Keep the training wheels off. Go to a museum. Hug life.
Walt, what are you saying?

Choose yes, he says, each new breath coming
slower and slower.
He jerks, squinches,
and a beeping sound
goes off.
Another nurse comes in
and does something
with his tubes.
This will help with the pain, she says.

Are you in pain?
I just got shot in the chest nine times, yo, he says, his eyes
rolling a little.

Actually, it was three.
Now's not the time to joke, Noah, he says, and then
squeezes

428

my hand tight,
and laughs heartily
like it's his last time
doing it.
For the first time
in our lives,
I see fear in
his eyes.
It's unmistakable.

Don't go, Walt. PLEASE! DON'T GO!

Walt Disney Jones listened to some good music, found cool, fell in love, took a hard swing at life, and then, because sometimes the world is not so beautiful, BAM!

I, Too?

Swing was born

the sun

in the center

exploding rays

of hope

to protect

the heart of

freedom

Walt Disney Jones

was shot

multiple times

by an officer

sworn

to keep peace in

our country,

from sea to shining sea.

Epilogue

Rare air, he flew
above possibility.

And, even though I know
that there will never be forevers

for wild birds, hunted
like game,

that there will never be forevers
for strange fruit

swinging in the breeze,
and even though I know

that America is sometimes
not so beautiful

and right
and just,

I know that Walt believed
that all the good in the world

could equate to an inch,
and he was convinced

he could grow it
into twenty thousand miles,

and he ran
with his head high, and his smile full,

base by base,
to make sure

that the good stretched out,
and he never stopped

talking about it
all the way home.

And I listened.
And I heard you, Swing.

And I hope you do too.

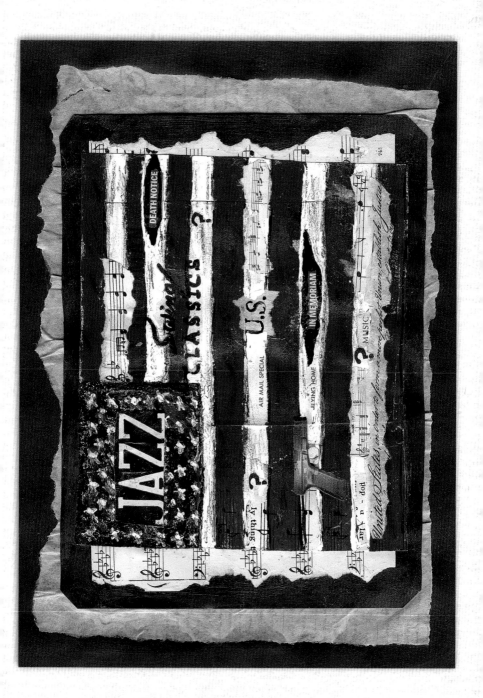

Check out this sample from
Kwame Alexander and Mary Rand Hess's
other novel, *Solo*, in stores everywhere!

By *New York Times* Bestselling Author

kwame
alexander

with Mary Rand Hess

There's this dream

I've been having
about my mother
that scares
the holy night
out of me,
and each time I wake
from it
I'm afraid to open
my eyes
and face
the world that awaits, the
fractured world
that used to make sense,
but now seems
disjointed—islands of possibility
that float by—like
a thousand puzzle pieces
that just don't fit
together anymore.

So I think
of Chapel
and grab hold
of the only other thing
that matters.
My guitar.

Strings

Mom used to play
this game
on the tour bus
to help us
go to sleep:

Who's the best?

We'd go through
every instrument:
piano, drums, horns.
Our favorite was guitar.

My sister, Storm, always said
Eddie Van Halen
was her favorite,
probably 'cause

he once made her
pancakes
at 4 am
in a Marriott kitchen.

Ask Rutherford and
he'd say,
I'm the best in the world,
I'm outta this world.
Electric soul brother interstellar man,
which is ironic
because he was trying
to quote
Lenny Kravitz, who

Mom would say
was in her top three
along with Jimi Hendrix
and me,
just to piss him off.

Chapel

is the great song
in my life.
The sweet arpeggio
in my solo.

Her lines bring
color and verve
to my otherwise
crazy life.

Without her
I'd be a one-man band,
with a played-out sound
and no audience.

The magic
we compose
is endless,
immortal.

We could play
together
for centuries.
If I'm lucky.

And I love
the music
our bodies
make
when we're dancing.

But there is one thing
about my girlfriend
I don't understand.
She says

she doesn't believe
in sex
before marriage,
but she never

wants to get married.
When I ask her, Where is this all going, then?
she likes to
get real close,

eyelash close,
and say things like
Let's live in the moment, babe
or *we don't need labels,*

and then
she kisses me
like we own the world
and nothing else matters.

It's funny how
going nowhere
feels like it's
going someplace

fast.

Texts from Chapel

7:37 pm
On your way stop by
Best Buy pls. Headphones broke.
Red or purple. K?

7:47 pm
They finally left. I
hate hiding. Wish my dad
wasn't so CRAY. He

7:48 pm
thinks all the things
the tabloids say
about your family

7:48 pm
are true. He doesn't know
you're different, Blade.
He says

7:48 pm
you're going to
drag me into sex
and drugs.

7:49 pm
Hurry up and get here.
They're at Bible study
'til 10 . . .

Leaving in ten minutes

Sorry. Working on a song.
Beats or *Bose*?
And tell the Reverend I
only did drugs once.

The Show

My father,
Rutherford Morrison,
can't stand
to be away
from the stage.
He has always craved
the spotlight,
needs it
like a drug,
posing, posturing, profiling
before millions—
an electric prophet, or so he thinks,
capturing concert worshipers
in the vapors
of his breath,
as if his voice
was preparing them
for rapture.

My sister and I
have always lived
under the stage,
beside it,
behind it.

The After-Party

There was always
another party.
More loud music.
More loud groupies.
Booze
and still more groupies.

I was nine.

He grabbed me
and held
a sizzling cig
in front
of my face.
Only it wasn't a cig.
He blew smoke
circles around me
and laughed.
My boy.

The band uncles got
in on the joke too,
and I stuck my tongue
in a shot glass
full of whiskey,
soaked it up
like a dirty sponge.
I loved making them laugh.

The whiskey hurt
my throat and
stung my eyes.
But the laughs
were epic.

Before I knew it

I was taking my finger
and dragging it
across powdered
sugar that looked
like ant snow trails
on the table.
Rutherford was too busy
kissing his ego
to notice.
I tasted it once,
twice, and
a few more times,
trying to find
that sugar sweet.

But, it wasn't sweet.
It was salty
bitter
and it coated
my mouth
in numbness.

I woke up
in the ICU
frightened
and embarrassed
by my father,
who sat by
my bedside
crying
in handcuffs.

Hollywood Report

Rutherford Morrison has kept rock alive for twenty-five
years.
His band, The Great Whatever, is credited with
introducing a new flavor of

Hard Rock to America with the release of their triple-
platinum album,
The History of Headaches. Even after an acrimonious
band breakup,

Morrison continued to have an illustrious solo career,
selling thirty million albums worldwide.

His music has lasted the test of time . . . until now.
Eight years ago, he was arrested for reckless
endangerment of his child,

and he hasn't released an album since.
Most recently he's managed three DUIs, and a drug
overdose

that almost sent him to a rock-star reunion with
Kurt Cobain and Amy Winehouse.

Rutherford may not have much time left before
he falls flat on 12:00. Midnight can be so cruel.

Who doesn't feel sorry for his kids,
left answering the hard questions, like

How does it feel
to be the daughter
to be the son
of a fallen rock star?

Who Am I?

I am
the wretched son
of a poor
rich man.

I do not hate
my life.

I am not like
Sebastian Carter,
who found
his father kissing
his girlfriend

and now hates
his life.

My life is, hmmm,
inconvenient.

But
if it weren't for Chapel ...

Are You Sure They Aren't Coming Home?

Chapel and I are about to take flight,
two souls on fire

burning through sacred mounds of
fresh desire.

Our lips are in the process
of becoming

one
in her hammock,

like two blue jays nesting.
Feeding each other

kisses of wonder.
I'm sure, she answers.

Hands of curiosity.
What are you doing?

Kissing you.
Slow down, Blade.

Why?
Woo me.

Woo you?
A song.

Come on, babe, we don't have time for that.
But we have time for this? she says,

puckering her lips, and
hypnotizing me

with eyes blue
as the deep blue sea.

Those Eyes Will Be the Death of Me

My gravestone will read:
Here lies a young man
who died inside
the gaze of a woman.

I watch the river
in her eyes gallop forth
fall into them
dive into them.

She smiles.
Those eyes.
I can't escape
the depth of them.

The song has ended,
but the melody still rings
from her mouth.
I can't hear a word.

I'm lost
in these two comets
that move across
my universe.

I remember
the first time
she looked at me
like this.

Two years ago

before he hit
an all-time low,
Rutherford threw
one of his

Hollywood Rocker House Parties
which became Storm's
pool party
SLASH sweet sixteen
SLASH get-all-the-kids-at-our-school-drunk-so-they-
could-listen-to-Storm's-mixtape-and-think-it-is-hot
party.

While they dove deep
in shallowness,
I found a quiet corner,
a vintage Rutherford Morrison guitar
took it off the wall
and started playing
American Woman
and any tune
with a hard groove
to soften
the dull.

Minutes
or an hour
went by
before I looked up,
and there she was
sitting
in the chair
across from me,
her legs

with dancer calves
entwined
like twin yellow flowers.
Her skin, amber sun.
And those pretty blue eyes
just watching me
like she cared.

Amazing. Keep playing, she said. *Don't let me interrupt
you.* And
then she got up,
sauntered off
glancing over her shoulder,
leaving me
thunderstruck.

Those eyes.
Those blue eyes.